The Summerhouse Project

For Margaret and
Gerry

— Richard

The Summerhouse Project

Cryptic Visions

Richard E Harding

Type set in Palatino Linotype 11 pt

ISBN 978-0-9574159-0-4

A CIP catalogue record for this book is available from the British Library

Written, edited, published and cover design by
Richard E Harding

Thanks to:

indoor • outdoor • anytime

for permission to use the summerhouse image

Copyright © 1999 - 2012 summerhouse image
Copyright © 2011 - 2012 Fifthroom logo image

www.fifthroom.com
5410 Route 8
Gibsonia, PA 15044
USA

Printed in the UK by Inky Little Fingers Ltd

For Gill
My first reader

The Summerhouse Project

The Summerhouse Project

CONTENTS

The Summerhouse Project

INTRODUCTION

NOVEL BEGINNINGS

One day I thought of an ending for a book which didn't yet exist, so I built up the story backwards! It gradually came together with ideas for a beginning and it sort of joined up somewhere in the middle, plugging in other chapter ideas which seemed necessary and relevant to glue the whole thing together.

This attempt to write a novel arose after accepting the challenge presented by the phrase: 'everyone has a novel inside them'. It was the mid 1980s and I had just completed a full-time science degree when I began writing about the concept of reality.

This fiction novel was an aside from the science writing which I undertook to write in parallel. After about a year I had finished the story and the resulting wad of type-written A4 sheets remained in a ring binder inside a cardboard box along with the science stuff for over a quarter of a century - until 2011 when I decided that I would try to rewrite the novel into a book. I hunted out a free OCR program from the internet and downloaded it - it was the perfect solution to the problem. Each page was scanned and run through the program to be auto-read and converted into editable text.

After many weeks of rewriting, deleting, correcting grammar, syntax, spelling mistakes and punctuation, I had the makings of a reasonable novel, although no-one had ever read it! The whole process was a bit like a sculptor with a roughly hewn block of stone from which some semblance of meaningful detail gradually emerged from laborious and painstaking chipping away at the endless irrelevant parts. The task of enduring re-reading and editing was by far the worst part of the whole business of producing a book from that typewritten manuscript.

The choice of cover design was to either go for a colourful eye-grabbing image and big title text, or as I did, for a subtle psychological symbolic approach with the blood red title symbolising murder and the black background the finality of death. The ghostly image of the summerhouse offers an opportunity for hope as a timeless window through to the past and out to the future.

I hope you enjoy the finished product despite any remaining mistakes!

Richard E Harding, August 2012

The Summerhouse Project

The Summerhouse Project

CHAPTER ONE

ALICE

Mark stepped from the train at Cambridge station. The journey from London had imparted to him a sense of calm, generated by leaving the big noisy city to then emerge into the rural approaches of Cambridge.

Returning to the city once more, he felt he had somehow come home. He thought back to his student days and the wonderful hot summer of seventy six. It was a city in which he could have spent the rest of his life, but his family back at Hampstead had looked forward to his homecoming. His parents, in particular his mother, wanted to show off their newly qualified son at those awful dinner parties she was so fond of organising. It was now six years on and he faced his most important job interview so far in his career.

His father had unexpectedly died after suffering a short illness and this had changed his mother's character completely. Alice could no longer cope with the things which had previously filled her life and which had come so easily to her. Her scores of friends and acquaintances who had once drunk port and champagne on the patio on summer evenings, talking about the latest scandal and where they would holiday that year, had all seemed to vanish into thin air. His mother had possessed a sort of magnetic ambience about her which seemed to attract a certain sort of person: the rich and famous, and those who knew absolutely everybody and anyone that mattered.

During the last two years or so since his father's untimely death, Alice had become almost a recluse, the total opposite of her former self. She used to always be happy, or at least appeared to be, and above all the centre of attraction. She was always an outgoing, supremely confident woman organising this and that, from bridge evenings to continental cruises - that memory now seemed like a dream to him.

Mark had lived with all of this and hated it. The lifestyle he was forced to lead was not at all to his liking; it was false with no sincerity, no real friends - except his uncle David. Mark had always suspected that he also disapproved of his sister's high-society lifestyle but nevertheless had always put on a brave face and joined in with the events, perhaps only for his wife's sake. Mark and David always got on well together, talking for hours on end about the things in life which interested them both. They would talk of one day getting away from it all to lead a quiet unhurried existence far from busy London.

Mark was burdened with the almost impossible task of helping his mother through the months after his father's death, but was unable to prevent her utter despair and deep depression which sometimes would carry on for weeks with little respite. She began taking to her bed for days at a time, with the little yellow pills being the only thing which allowed her to keep going, if that was what it was, but certainly no life for either of them. During these times Mark had to give up any ideas of a career for which he had worked so hard to secure.

Alice had two sons. Mark's brother, John, didn't come to his father's funeral. He had set up a practice in New Zealand after many years at college and medical school at Cambridge, long before Mark decided to follow in his medical footsteps. The busy surgery, situated on the outskirts of Auckland, had left him short of time to return to England to attend the funeral. John had said in one of his communications, that one day he would meet Mark in Cambridge and they would travel down to London together. It would help to soften the emotion of him seeing his mother a changed person after last being with her in buoyant mood at his send-off party to the other side of the world.

Although his brother had qualified as a general practitioner, Mark had always had a dream ambition to become a surgeon, while his school chums were going to become airline pilots or politicians. It was probably something to do with his privileged middle-class roots, which in fact he was far from proud. Although he had also studied at Cambridge, Mark had not wanted to be a family doctor, but instead, had specialised in neurology and had spent his time at some of London's hospitals gradually gaining experience in the technical side of the subject as new instrumentation and patient monitoring methods were fast improving.

He had spent so much time at different bedsides and operating tables with the patients plugged in to the EEG and ECG monitors that at times he really wondered if he had taken the right direction in his medical career. In a great many cases the patient was kept alive artificially on life support machines, but the brain activity always gave a feeling of hope that the person may show signs of improvement and eventually become well again to make it all worthwhile.

Mark would often sit quietly after dinner at his Hampstead home wondering if his chosen vocation was the right one. A person who may desperately need his skills could be lying there wired-up to the machines. He was sure he was doing a very worthwhile job as the sheer joy of a patient's recovery was something wonderful to behold. He often thought of his father at times like this and how things could have been had he regained his health.

He found it hard to control his emotions when recovery from brain damaged road accident victims occurred, most especially with the children. He loved the children, and to Mark, the child in the bed could be his own child, and he sometimes imagined it was. He realised the great hazard of a doctor's job was not to become emotionally involved with his patients. He had to face the problem of having to hide, and somehow suppress the real emotions he felt; this he knew he had to do in order to succeed.

*   *   *

It was one of those mornings when he thought to himself that he desperately needed a break, a different daily routine, but lately most mornings he had thought like that. He glanced over to the letter basket to see a large white envelope. It didn't seem that long ago that he had waited at the bottom of the stairs as a child eager for his birthday or Christmas cards to arrive into the very same gilded cage. Over the past few weeks he had been idly thumbing through the job sections of medical magazines and the internal information sheets at the hospitals he visited and had applied for a few of them. This particular correspondence concerned a position for which he was offered an interview. This news immediately made the day seem like a day he could cope with anything that was thrown at him. It was a vacancy for a neurology technician at Addenbrooke's hospital in Cambridge. The very thought of living and working in that wonderful city again lifted his spirits.

He had an immediate problem - Alice. Although his mother had a daily help to arrange for cleaning, meals and washing, how could he leave his mother and live in another city? He pondered as to whether he should attend the interview, but quickly decided he must; it was a chance not to miss. That same day, without a word to anyone, he confirmed the interview date by phone - a week and a day to go! But what was he going to do about Alice?

His uncle David had been calling on regular visits to his sister to try and cheer her up and it seemed to be working. He had been able to coax her from her bed or armchair and out into the large, now overgrown garden. Mark had fond memories of this high-walled garden with its apple orchard and sweeping lawn where his mother once played croquet with her cronies. The lawn was rarely cut now and the apple orchard was left to itself, but the garden still held the magic it had for him as a child. He and John were always to be found in the summerhouse discussing Mark's latest invention. Summerhouses have a timeless quality once you step inside, like a time machine.

David turned up a day earlier than his usual day for visiting Alice, he couldn't wait to tell her some good news that he hoped she *would* receive as good news. He took her into the garden and held her arm until they had walked to the summerhouse. Mark followed behind as they chatted about one thing and another and how David and Rosemary's family were getting on. They had one daughter who had left home at an early age to seek her fortunes elsewhere. They heard from her occasionally, and her letters were full of what she was going to do next; at least she had a spirited, ambitious approach to life.

She very rarely paid her parents a visit and on one occasion mentioned casually in a letter that she had married an estate agent she had been living with for some months before. It hurt her family that she hadn't invited anyone to the wedding, but Suzy was that kind of girl. She went about her business in her own independent way, no family ties and no responsibilities. But she did shock everyone by turning up at her uncle's funeral and then disappearing without so much as a word to anyone. She had always shown a special affection for her uncle and had visited him and Alice almost weekly as a child. Strangely, the summerhouse held a fascination for her too.

Mark and uncle David helped the now frail Alice up the three bricked steps and onto the moss covered boards of the summerhouse. It had seen better days, but was oddly beautiful and serene. It had become draped with ivy and had two rhododendron bushes at either side of the steps, almost engulfing them in their overgrowth as if to seal the entrance to the structure. Behind the summerhouse stood two poplar trees, like timeless guardian sentinels. Mark helped his mother over to one of the ancient fraying white-painted wicker chairs and David was staring up towards the house as the conversation ceased. He turned on his heel.

"Alice, I have a proposition; come and live with us. You can have Suzanne's old room overlooking the park, you know how much you said you loved it there."

Both Mark and David waited for her decision.

"Well, what do you think?" asked David, not having received a reply. Alice burst into floods of tears.

"Whatever's the matter mother? Don't you think it's a marvellous idea?"

He thought of Cambridge, and how this was a solution to his problem and to Alice's loneliness. It was almost as if in that magical summerhouse his dear uncle David knew his problem. Alice looked up at their concerned faces, wiping the tears from her cheeks.

"My house, my wonderful garden. I can't, I can't . . ." She sobbed bitterly for many minutes, Mark and David unable to console her.

"But why not Alice? We would love to have you, and you'd be good company for Rosemary when I'm away on business."

David and Mark both looked at each other concerned, for it would solve quite a few problems.

Alice gave voice through her sobs.

"I know you mean well, but I can't leave my beautiful house; it holds so many cherished memories for me."

"All right!" David replied firmly. "Rosemary will live here and look after you. I know she wouldn't mind; she said you would never leave here."

Alice was strangely quiet for a few moments and then agreed amidst a resurgence of tears - tears of relief and happiness for once in a very long time.

"It would be so kind of Rosemary."

"That's settled then," said David. "I will arrange for Rosemary's things to be brought over in the morning if that's all right with you Alice? You won't go and change your mind now will you?" He smiled and gave her a good hug.

"You are so very kind David, and thank Rosemary for me won't you - now don't forget."

"As if I would. Rosemary will look forward to a change of environment anyway; twenty years she's been in that house you know, the change will be good for her."

Mark listened to all that was said, but the words seemed to drift past him as he could only think of his interview in a few days time. He loved his mother, but convinced himself that with Rosemary there to look after things and David popping in and out with the shopping and the occasional car trip out somewhere, that Alice would be in good hands.

Arm-in-arm, they all walked back towards the house which looked down on them as if to welcome their presence inside once more. The house stood well back from the quiet cul-de-sac in its own grounds with a curved gravelled driveway. Tall sycamores almost hid it from view, except for the small attic window which was Mark's room.

Over the days which followed Rosemary's arrival at the house, everything went well. Mark plucked up courage, and after a brief word with Rosemary, told his mother of his plans and hopes for the job, should he be lucky enough to get it! As it turned out they were both pleased for him and knew that if he lived in Cambridge he would write home regularly and pay them a visit whenever he could. He would miss the old place.

The day before the interview Mark arrived home earlier than usual as he needed time to think out the arrangements and what he would say at the interview the following day. The train journey would be simple enough and his appointment was at eleven o'clock. After breakfast his taxi arrived.

"Right ladies," he announced. "It's time I was on my way!"

"You'll get your job all right don't you worry about that my lad," Alice said triumphantly, as if she had arranged the whole thing without him knowing. Aunt Rosy nodded in agreement. Alice was always optimistic for others just lately, but never for herself. Perhaps this would change now she had a companion once again.

CHAPTER TWO

INTERVIEW

As Mark took the bus from Cambridge station he decided that once the interview was over he would travel into the city centre to visit his old college of St. Johns. But first the interview.

Addenbrooke's hospital swung into view as he peered through the bus window and in the space of the next couple of minutes he stood staring at the multitude of windows which confronted him. He had prepared himself as to what *not* to say, which, in his opinion was far more important than what he did say. His experience would stand him in good stead, with lots of references he had collected from the London hospitals and research departments he had worked in. A smart new grey suit provided the finishing touches. He had decided not to shave off his beard as it just wasn't him without it. Besides, he had first grown it when his college won an important rugby match, despite the pouring rain!

Once inside, he asked for directions at one of the numerous clinic desks and a young blonde nurse insisted on taking him right to the very entrance to the department. He wasn't too sure he was ready for such a dramatic entry.

"Here we are," she announced.

He thanked her, and with a quick glance at his watch confirmed it was ten to eleven. He had taken note of the time at every clock he passed on his way through the corridors. He caught the attention of a passing nurse.

"Could you please tell me where I might find Dr. Bruensen . . . neurology department please?" he said.

"Yes, certainly. You go through the double doors," she gesticulated, "and take the left-hand corridor, and about halfway down on the left is his secretary's office," she explained.

He made his way to the allotted door, labelled 'Miss Rogers'. He gave a confident knock and a voice permeated into the corridor from within. Upon opening the door the secretary invited him in to take a seat. Mark closed the door behind him and sat next to a smartly dressed older gentleman.

"Are you here for eleven o'clock?" Mark asked.

"No," he replied hesitantly, obviously nervous. "Eleven-thirty it says in my letter." He produced the letter and stuck a finger under the stated time as if to convince himself as much as Mark.

All Mark was concerned about was that this other fellow wasn't before him if they were running a bit late with the interviews. He couldn't bear the thought of waiting longer than another five minutes let alone thirty or however long it would take.

"Mr. James," came Miss Rogers' trained voice.

Mark jerked to his feet.

"Yes, thank you," he politely replied, trying to look calmer than he felt.

Miss Rogers led him through her office and in through another door which was Dr. Bruensen's office. A man in a charcoal-grey suit stood behind a desk with his arm outstretched. As Mark shook his hand firmly, Miss Rogers retired to her office.

"Good morning. Dr. James is it not? Mark, I believe," he boomed.

"Yes, it is. How do you do?"

"Very well, very well," he repeated. "Do have a seat."

Now, in situations like interviews there are usually two seats to choose from, and Mark's quick mind knew it was a standard psychological trap and that it mattered which seat he chose - he was certain of it - but with very little time to make a calculated decision he sat on the nearest seat to where he stood. He thought that must have been correct as it indicated a quick decision maker, no hesitation there.

"Oh! Sorry about the chair," Bruensen suddenly said. "The back's completely gone, or very nearly - needs to go down to the workshop you know. Sorry about that . . . completely slipped my mind." Mark leapt to his feet and plonked himself down in the other seat thinking 'so much for psychology!'

"Well, Mark, why do you feel particularly suited for this position?" he enquired rather cryptically.

Mark went sailing through all his experience and qualifications trying to add subtle extra emphasis when a well known department or person was mentioned. He was suddenly stopped mid-breath.

"Fine, fine," repeated Bruensen. "Now! How about accommodation? In the city is it?"

Mark floundered and muttered something about it probably *would* be in the city, not daring to contradict.

"When will I know if I am to be offered the position sir?" He tried to sound confident.

"Damn it man, I've given you the job!" he boomed again. "Now, the important thing is when can you start?"

"Oh! Thank you . . . that's great," replied Mark, hardly believing his ears. "Monday, if that's all right with you sir."

"Monday's fine. We'll meet in this office at eight-thirty sharp. I'll show you around the place and then you can get started . . . unless you would like to have a look around now - before you definitely decide. You might not like the colour scheme!" he guffawed.

"No, no, that's fine, I'll see you Monday then."

He was beginning to speak like him. Oh! God, what if he couldn't help unconsciously copying him - the way he repeats himself, Mark agonised.

"Well, thank you again," he said, making for the door.

He opened it and closed it behind him, leaning on it

with a feeling of utter relief. When he opened his eyes, he found himself face to face with Miss Rogers.

"Oh! Sorry, this way is it?" He coughed and laughed all at the same time and headed for the way out.

"Everything OK? Did the interview go well," she enquired.

"Yes thank you, fine, fine. I got the job."

The Summerhouse Project

CHAPTER THREE

JANE

Mark decided that he had no time to pay a visit to his old college, but needed to quickly find somewhere to live. He took the bus in the general direction of bed-sit land after finding out the area from a group of nurses at the bus-stop which had saved him time; he needed to find a place pretty quick.

He found a great many likely streets between the hospital and the city centre. He really needed a flat, a bed-sit was too small and not permanent enough. After asking at various places he eventually spoke to a few people living in a flat in Bateman street, quite near to the rail station. They said they knew the flat next door had recently been vacated and that the landlady was the same as theirs. A telephone call to the landlady in question proved fruitful and she could meet him later that day. In the meantime he was asked in for coffee by the group he had spoken with. During the course of the conversation it turned out that two Addenbrooke's nurses lived next door in the same block with the vacancy - one male, the other female.

At just after four in the afternoon a little red mini pulled up outside and out stepped the landlady. Mark bounded down the stairs to meet her.

"Hello! I'm Mark James about the flat," he said breathlessly.

"Yes, the previous tenant left at short notice."

After a quick chat, Mark produced the job letter letter.

"That's OK - the flat's yours if you want it; now let me show you around."

"OK, that's great. I'll be working at the hospital - the same as your tenants here already - quite a coincidence really I suppose," he said beaming at his good fortune.

The landlady nodded.

"You're a good bunch."

He thanked her and made an advance payment to secure the flat and tucked the key in his pocket. What a stroke of luck, he thought as he made his way back to the rail station - a job and a flat all in one day. At least he didn't have to worry about where to live, which would leave his mind clear for the challenge of his new job.

*   *   *

Rosemary and Alice were fast asleep on his return late that night, and after fixing himself a snack and coffee, gently woke Rosemary to break the good news. She was as thrilled as he was and made a beeline for the kettle. They let Alice sleep as it was quite late by now; the pills she took made her so tired.

Rosemary plonked herself down on a kitchen stool.

"Well, what did you find out about the job?" she asked excitedly.

"I start straight away this Monday, I couldn't believe it would be so soon. I don't feel prepared - and guess what? I'm fixed up with a flat too!" Mark enthused. "It's quite near to the station and within easy reach of the hospital!"

At that moment Alice woke up. She was still drowsy from the medication but called out in the direction of the voices.

"Rosemary, is that you talking to someone?"

"Yes, it's Mark, and he's got some good news about his job. Oh! We must have woken her," she whispered to Mark. "I'd better nip in and see if she's all right as she acts a bit strangely if she wakes suddenly - sort of bewildered."

They both went in to tell Alice all about the news and Mark apologised for waking her so late. Alice didn't seem to take it in, so Mark said he'd tell her in the morning. Over breakfast Mark explained everything to his mother, but noticed by her eyes that all was not well with her. Alice said very little that day and Rosemary guessed why: she couldn't bear the thought of her other son leaving home. She never saw John and it was obvious that she had the same thoughts about Mark despite his previous reassurance.

Sunday soon came around, and for most of the day Mark was packing everything he thought he might need. Alice was fussing around like a mother hen and he felt sorry for her, but it was now *his* turn to do something exciting with his life. He spent most of the afternoon packing his computer together with bits and pieces of electronic gadgetry. Electronics had been his hobby ever since his father had brought home an old radiogram and they got it working between them. When he was about fifteen his interest moved to electric guitars, building them and using the radiogram's amplifier to play them through.

His attic bedroom was a tangle of multicoloured wires with labels which said where they all went. The room hadn't changed much over the following years but his electronic expertise certainly had; he had become the proverbial whiz-kid. He naturally looked out for jobs involving electronics and medical instrumentation which he'd studied extensively whilst at college. His new job was like a dream come true and would involve the exciting prospect of computer applications.

*　*　*

Uncle David had kindly offered to run him and his gear to Cambridge after he had changed the oil in his ageing Hillman estate. When the time came and the last item of luggage was safely aboard, it was tears at the gate with Alice sniffling on Rosemary's shoulder. Mark had half expected it bearing in mind his mother's condition, but he knew she would be well looked after thanks to David and Rosemary's wonderful generosity. As they turned following the driveway to the road, Mark waved again and settled down for the journey. It was David who spoke first. Mark was unaware he was thinking over various things creating a long silence.

"Everything OK then Mark?"

"Yes. Oh, yes fine. Sorry, I was thinking about the garden and the summerhouse when John and I were kids. You often came to visit us and we really had some good times together - with dad too."

"They *were* good times, I often think of them too. I simply love that garden. It has a strange quality about it - sort of hauntingly serene - a kind of retreat from the bustle of the real world. That sounds rather profound doesn't it, but I felt it when we were in the summerhouse with Alice, something which is difficult to describe really." He glanced over to Mark.

"You've described it perfectly, I feel it too," Mark said excitedly. "Why is it do you think? I thought it was only me who felt that about the garden - and in particular the summerhouse."

David stared at the road ahead.

"I don't quite know what it is Mark," he said cryptically. "Cambridge sounds a good place to work," he said, changing the subject rather abruptly. "Quite the centre for science and medicine I understand. What exactly will you be doing at the hospital?" David enquired.

Mark had to tear his thoughts away from the image of the garden before he could think to answer.

"It's all to do with bedside monitoring equipment for brain-damaged patients and comes under the heading of medical physics and there's ongoing research into new ways to help understand the patient's condition while unconscious in a coma. It's a whole new challenge - looking into people's brains so to speak. I've learnt a lot about the subject and the latest monitoring devices at the London hospitals," Mark explained to his rather perplexed uncle.

"It sounds as if it's right up your street Mark - electronics and all that, you should do well."

"I hope so."

Mark gazed out of the window thinking about his college days again, and the fun they had, like the time a whole gang of them took out four punts and took them right through to Grantchester meadows side by side forcing all the other punts out of the way. They had ended up at The Orchard tea garden in Grantchester village where the church clock stood at ten-to-three! It was so real to him reliving that afternoon that he let out a chuckle. David turned and smiled.

After arriving and unpacking all of Mark's things, David left almost immediately, politely refusing a cup of coffee and mentioning something about sorting out some books. During that Sunday evening Mark spent a lot of the time setting up his newly acquired computer on a convenient large table under the window - a good light for any soldering jobs he thought to himself. He was about to retire for the night after a quick meal out of tins, when a knock sounded at his hallway door. A young lady stood at the door and explained she was from the flat above his. She asked if he was all right for everything.

"Yes, thank you, I think I'm pretty well sorted out. It's been quite a day with all the packing and unpacking." He hung on the door frame looking as if he was all in.

"I hear you're starting at Addenbrooke's. I'm a nurse there and so is my boyfriend," she gestured towards upstairs. He thought some guys have all the luck! She was incredibly attractive and it took all of his concentration to take in what she was saying. He certainly sensed a mutual attraction between them but was too exhausted to cope with anything else that day.

"I start Monday," he said, "in the neurological physics department." She looked surprised.

"Oh, I thought you were going to be a ward doctor."

"I am a doctor, but I sort of drifted away from that into more specialised work in medical physics - you know, all those boxes with flashing lights, EEG and ECG monitoring equipment and stuff. That's what I've got to look after, and there's a whole bunch of research projects to run too, so there's certainly lots to do."

"They get a lot of road accident cases in there I'm told, quite horrific I should imagine." She gave a little wince. "I've yet to do my stint in there," she said, biting her bottom lip. Mark could feel his legs almost giving way under him, he had to get some sleep.

"I might see you around then," he said. "What's your name?"

"Jane, Jane Ryder," she said looking slightly embarrassed.

"Pleased to meet you, Jane Ryder! I'm Mark. I've just moved here from London and I'm sure I'll find Cambridge a stimulating place to work."

His hand grasped the door knob as he thanked her and closed the door. It was nearly midnight and he fell into bed.

CHAPTER FOUR

COMATOSE

Monday morning he took the bus straight to the hospital and was shown around the department by Dr. Bruensen. He was introduced to the other doctors and staff and then told of the patients he would be involved with. At the time there were five cases: three had been there for a good many weeks and the other two had been admitted on the last two consecutive evenings. All had been identified bar one. This was a middle-aged man who had been the victim of a hit-and-run near the city centre and he carried no identification. The police had called in to question him on a couple of occasions, but the man had remained unconscious. He had severe head injuries, a broken right leg and fractures to his right forearm and the car driver was unknown.

The only witness who came forward was a woman who was waiting at the Cambridge bus stop quite near to the scene of the accident. She remembered the man walking rather jerkily and looking behind him a few times. Then it all happened so quickly: a large dark car, as she described it, turned the corner to her right, out of Downing street. It had taken the corner very wide, almost over to the far side of the main street. It was quite late in the evening and few other cars or pedestrians were about.

The car continued in a wide circle and mounted the pavement about ten yards beyond her, hitting the man as he began running, as if he was expecting it to happen. She then said the man crumpled over the nearside wing of the car and was flung over with considerable force, hitting his head on the pavement. Her statement to the police continued: She said the strange thing was, the car certainly didn't seem out of control and appeared to hit him intentionally; it only just missed her at the bus stop. The car then sped away, turning right into Emmanuel street towards the bus station.

Another person, who by now had come across the scene, was a young lad and it was he who had phoned for the ambulance from the box just across the road. She ended her statement by saying that a small group of people had gathered around the stricken man, thought to be dead. This was the only eye-witness account of what had happened. The woman had insisted on travelling with the man to the hospital where she gave police and doctors the full story.

The whole case of this mystery man and his assailants intrigued Mark, who was told the sequence of events by the doctor who had received him in casualty; he was then taken to see the man. Monitoring electrodes sprouted from his head and chest attached to the EEG and ECG machines. A massive contusion on the man's temple was being attended to by a nurse; he had just survived - only just. As Mark well knew, the next twenty-four hours were crucial. All that week he was assigned to this patient, taking care to note down any changes in his condition shown by the monitors. The man survived the critical period, but would probably exist only in a life of unconsciousness. Could there be a chance that he might recover and be able to solve the mystery? He hoped so.

The police only called once more as it was obvious that the man was not in any position to be of help. The next day the mystery patient and all the equipment were moved into a private room where Mark was able to concentrate on the emerging paper printouts from the two main monitors: one for various brain functions and the other for heart response. A nurse came in three times a day to provide liquid nourishment via a nasal tube to his stomach. A careful watch was also made on his blood glucose levels by taking blood samples twice a day. The police asked to be contacted if he was in any state to communicate with them, obviously it seemed most unlikely as things stood.

It was exactly a week since Mark had started work at the hospital when he began to notice a small detail on the man's CRT monitor waveform. All the information was produced as a hard copy on graph paper so it could be scrutinised at leisure, but he went straight to it as it churned out of the printer. They were there! He hadn't imagined them as he feared from hours of staring at the readouts.

What he had seen he couldn't make sense of, they just should not be there. He certainly hadn't seen anything like it in all his months of training in London. The normal brain function modulations definitely showed a parasitic secondary inflexion on the amplitude waveform - a small wave within a wave. As he had never come across anything like it before, Mark thought it wise to check all the equipment and connections to the patient, although he was sure it couldn't be that as the pattern was too regular and only appeared on the ascending limbs of the waveform. He decided not to mention it to Dr. Bruensen - it was a problem he wanted to sort out for himself. Once he had done that, he could explain it to him; but what on earth was causing it?

One evening he was lying on his bed back at the flat thinking over how this phenomenon could possibly occur. It was then that he remembered that it was only occurring at certain periods during the day. He leapt up and stared out the window across the chimney pots, positively locked in deep thought. Suddenly he realised it was only happening during REM sleep, the times when a person is dreaming, causing the eyes to move around under the lids. What was he dreaming about? That was the crucial question. He could be reliving his recent past and the solution to the mystery could be locked away in his head!

Mark began to think of his experience with computers at the London hospitals. Whenever he had the time, he set about trying to solve the problem of somehow interpreting these micro-modulations. The first step was obvious, well at least to him. He needed to amplify the small waveforms into a larger, more detailed image. Within a fortnight he held in his hand a device, which according to his calculations should link to the electroencephalograph output to produce a greatly amplified signal. More than that - it would also record them as a digitised signal on magnetic tape.

It became a familiar sight within the department to see Mark lugging various pieces of equipment to and from the physics lab and into the neurology ward, so it was absolutely no problem for him to bring his black box device in to work . During a reasonably quiet period in the ward, Mark tested out his device suitably wired up to the stranger's EEG readout terminals. In fact he could have done it at any time because his projects were virtually unintelligible to anyone else. It was his guilty conscience niggling at him because he hadn't told Bruensen or anyone else about what he was doing.

Through headphones, he could hear the evidence that his device did actually work - the REM sleep micro-modulations were now stored in his device. He had some data now which he could get to work on back at the flat. He decided he would leave his box connected for as long as possible for each of the REM sleep periods of dreaming. Mark managed to collect what must have been hours of data and the next stage was to decode the signals into a more useful state. That meant spending long hours in the physics department's library hunting for some computer aided means to transpose data in digital form which could then be explored in more detail than it ever could be in its raw EEG state.

CHAPTER FIVE

THE PROJECT

Most evenings when Mark wasn't required at the hospital were spent scribbling out different program ideas, none of which were working out. He would very often fall asleep over his sheets of A4 only to wake in the early hours aching all over and then having to drag himself into the bedroom to try and snatch some sleep. It was turning out to be just one of those evenings and he felt himself about to give in to nodding off when a rap at his door made him jerk suddenly back into the land of the living. He found the door just in time to see his upstairs neighbour about to ascend the stairs. He had quite forgotten how pretty she was.

"Hello," he yelled.

"I'd come down to see if you were all right," she said in a concerned voice. "I can usually hear you moving about, but it's been so quiet just lately I was worried."

"That's very kind of you to be concerned, thanks. Won't you come in for a cup of sugar or something," he quipped.

43

The Summerhouse Project

It had been so long since he had spoken to anyone socially that Mark was determined to make an effort, it might be the only thing which would preserve his sanity.

"Yes I will come in, but I'm afraid I won't be needing any sugar!"

She came down the stairs and into his very untidy room.

"My God! Whatever do you do down here?"

Mark gave a half-hearted laugh.

"It *is* rather jumbled in here, I'd not really noticed before."

"Hey! You're into computers - great stuff!" she said enthusiastically and walked over to his desk perusing the piles of paperwork.

"I haven't seen you around the hospital; where are you working at the moment?" asked Mark.

"Oh, you wouldn't have, I'm right over the back of the site in maternity."

"It's Jane isn't it?" he remembered at last.

"Yes, and you're Mark," she said, looking up from the computer. "What on earth is all this work about? You ought to get out and enjoy yourself in the evenings you know, it's not good for you to stay in working."

"I know, but this project seems to be taking up every minute of my time just lately - it's become a sort of obsession; I feel I must finish it and find the truth." He immediately realised he'd not meant to say that.

"Truth! What truth? You sound like a whole weird

44

kind of guy!"

"No, it's not like that at all, it's all very complicated and difficult to explain."

"Try me!"

"What?"

"Try me. I like complicated things that are difficult to explain." She sat down on an old armchair.

"I don't know whether I should tell you." He felt uncomfortable and embarrassed; he hadn't intended to ever get into the awkward position of explaining his secret project to anyone.

"You can certainly trust me if that's the problem, I love keeping secrets," she said convincingly.

"Well I do feel I need someone to talk to about it, but . . ." Jane interrupted him with a complete reassurance that she had no intention of discussing private matters with anyone else. "But what about your boyfriend? He might object to you spending time here with me. I'm sure *I* would in the same circumstances," declared Mark.

"Steve doesn't live with me any more, I chucked him out three days ago. I just got so incredibly bored with him. All he could talk about was bloody football and how marvellous he was at his job. We had a blazing row in a restaurant and I just walked out telling the whole place that he was to collect his things and get out of my life! They cheered!"

"That sounds a bit drastic, you might want him back," he said with his fingers crossed behind his back.

"There's no way I'll want him back, thank you very much. I can't imagine what I ever saw in him to tell you the truth."

"You sound very sure about it."

"I bloody well *am* sure. Right!"

"OK. So now your interested in my little mystery," he remarked, at the same time trying to decide whether to confide in her or not. "It may be very boring as it's also to do with my job."

"What's to do with your job?" she asked insistently.

Mark thought that perhaps he shouldn't make it out to be so secret and mysterious, it was just that he wanted to get some positive results before he told Bruensen rather than make a fool of himself pursuing a most improbable, if not impossible project.

"Right Jane I'll tell you, but," he warned, "you must promise not to laugh."

"But I like to laugh. In fact I haven't had a good laugh for ages," she teased.

"And you won't tell a soul?"

"Not a soul", she promised.

Mark spent the rest of the evening and part of the night explaining to Jane exactly what he hoped to achieve. To his amazement, it turned out that she had a physics degree and soon understood his idea. He had thought she wouldn't grasp any of it and so he thought he was quite safe to tell her. She explained that although she had been to college, she had decided to take up nursing instead through a sense of duty.

The Summerhouse Project

Jane had looked after her mother for two years while she was dying of a muscular wasting complaint and it was whilst she was away at college, in between visits, that she had died. Although she carried on and finished her degree she couldn't come to terms with the fact that her mother had died during her absence and as a result carried with her the burden of guilt. It seemed the right thing to do, to enter nursing as a way to appease her guilt by helping others who were suffering illness.

Mark had listened intently to all of this and felt great sympathy and understanding. His thoughts went to his own father. He had been far closer to him than he ever was to his mother, but now looked upon Alice as a completely different person to how she was before his father's death. Her loss was too much for her to bear and she had simply crumpled up into the sad sight she was today. He must visit home sooner rather than later he decided.

Jane stayed the night - it was inevitable - they had so much in common. Over the next few weeks they grew closer and Mark was actually persuaded to go out to the hospital disco with her and really enjoy himself. He felt as happy as he used to be in his student years - in fact happier. The landlady didn't object to Jane giving up her flat, as there was no problem in obtaining another tenant. Mark's flat was bigger by virtue of a small box room, so they chose to live there.

Of course this meant Mark had a mass of clearing up to do and only he knew which papers he had no further use for and could throw out. He carefully tore all the old notes into small pieces before they went to the dustbin, and with Jane's help and her eye for décor, Mark hardly recognised the place; he now had more room to live and work.

After scores of attempts, Mark came up with a program which he was happy with. If it did what it was designed to do, it would take Mark's stored black box digital data of the EEG sub-modulations and convert them a section at a time into a video format. The hope was that with a bit of luck and a bit more tinkering about, the original REM sleep data would display itself on a video monitor. Could he really do it? Could he actually record and play back a person's thoughts and dreams? He knew that if it *did* work, he would be the first to do it. Jane was able to borrow a video recorder from the social club until it was needed in a week or so for the social club's film evening. Every spare moment they had was devoted to 'The Project'.

Mark told Jane about his life and she hers. He told her about the strange but wonderful garden at his mother's home in Hampstead and about the summerhouse. Mark promised her that when he went on one of his visits to see Alice he would take her along, especially to see the summerhouse and the garden. Jane admitted to Mark that she had often felt that she may somehow be in tune with things paranormal and that it would be interesting to find out if she felt anything there. Mark was now in the final stages of wiring up his masterpiece.

The Summerhouse Project

"You know," said Jane, chomping on an enormous cheese sandwich, "you ought to call this project: 'The Summerhouse Project'."

"Why? What's it got to do with the summerhouse?" queried Mark, tipping his head to one side.

"Don't you see the connection? You say that the summerhouse gives you the feeling that it somehow, in a paranormal sort of way, may hold secret memories within its ambience, just in the same way that poor guy's memories are likely to be held in your box."

"That's a very cool analogy Jane," Mark commented, wishing he'd thought of it. "I like it. Yes, very good!"

"Well, when's the big moment going to be? You said it would all be ready yesterday."

"Nearly there. I had the wrong plugs for the computer input yesterday, but I've sorted it all out now," he stated triumphantly amidst a cloud of vapourised solder flux. "I've managed to convert some other plugs so they'd fit OK."

"And do they, Einstein?"

"Well of course, Lady Jane!"

The Summerhouse Project

CHAPTER SIX

CRYPTIC VISIONS

Mark fiddled for ages with his soldering iron. "Everything's all wired up," he said proudly. "Shall I light the blue touch paper and retire?" he joked.

"Why not? I'd be most surprised if this Heath Robinson affair actually worked anyway!"

"Now that's not a very nice thing to say after all the work we've put into it."

Before them on the dining table stood a baffling array of boxes, gadgets, plugs and wires, all connected up to Mark's PC, the social club's VCR and a VDU monitor screen. Mark sent the first of the collected data through his program to the computer. He checked everything else was switched on and ready to go - the tape was set into motion. With bated breath they both stared at the screen. Nothing. They looked at each other and laughed, but they didn't mean it. It was the reaction which came spontaneously after months of toil, they could just as easily have burst into tears. Mark leapt to his feet and fiddled with a disk drive behind the computer.

"Thank God for that!" he gasped, visibly shaken.

"Why? What happened?"

"It's all right, don't panic Jane."

"Don't panic! It's you who panicked, remember?" she yelled accusingly. "Anyway, what was it?"

"The program. I forgot to load in the transposing program from the disk," he admitted, breathless from the leap.

"What now? Shouldn't it be doing something by now?" Jane was disappointed, she really thought it would work despite her earlier remark. She sighed back into the armchair thinking of coffee.

"Look!"

"What?"

"On the screen. Look!"

Jane tried to focus her eyes to the appropriate distance in all of a split second.

"What is it? It's just squiggles," she said, wondering what the excitement was all about.

"They *are* squiggles! It means it's working all right," explained Mark, rolling his eyes to the ceiling when Jane wasn't looking.

In that stupid moment he realised how much she really meant to him. He was sure he must love her; if only he had more time to think of her and their happiness just being together.

The screen cleared a bit to reveal what could only be described as fast flashing images. No detail could be made out at all. It was like masses of sticks and splodges moving at speed across the monitor screen. Mark stared at the wall for a few moments, sensing what was wrong or what *could* be wrong. He finally uttered and looked at Jane, who was lost in thought.

"If you're dreaming," he said intently, "what do you see?" He was on the edge of the chair. "It's fast isn't it? What you see in dreams is usually appearing to happen faster than the real world. You sort of go through a bit and then skip past a lot of it quickly don't you?"

"I'd never thought about it before, but yes, I think you're right," she nodded in agreement.

"So, if what we're seeing on the screen is a real dream sequence but a sort of speeded-up version, then if we slow the computer program down . . . no, that wouldn't work. What we have to do is to slow up the original signal recording from the EEG amplifier - I'm sure that must work."

Mark's mind was working at full tilt by now. There came a lull in activity as Mark began searching through half-a-dozen as yet unpacked large boxes of his electronic bits and pieces. Jane sneaked out the room making straight for the kettle while Mark rummaged and mumbled his way through the boxes. As Jane walked in the door with their coffees, Mark gave a yelp of delight clutching a most insignificant box.

"This should do it, it's worked before on one of my projects," he exclaimed. "You know what I'm going to do, don't you?"

"Yep! You're going to run the EEG data stream slower

so that the picture on the screen runs slower," she answered quickly.

"You're not just a pretty face are you?"

"No!"

At eight minutes to one in the morning he was ready again, with Jane fast nodding off. Mark started the sequence once again and the result was startling: trees, what looked like buildings of some sort and a jiggling frame affair all jumped around the screen. He slowed the stream some more. He was actually witnessing something no one on Earth, to his knowledge, had ever seen before. It seemed to be this guy's memory of a train journey. Mark carefully switched off the equipment as he felt tiredness overwhelm him. He shook poor Jane awake and together they headed for a well earned sleep. He would wait until the morning to tell Jane the incredible news and just before he fell asleep he thought of the miles of data yet to run.

*   *   *

The next day Jane had the morning off duty so Mark didn't wake her, but he did leave her a note to say that he had seen some pictures which he could hardly believe were there before his eyes. That evening they began again, trying to scrutinise every scrap of information they saw. When Jane first saw the images she looked over to Mark's excited face with a blank look on hers, but was soon convinced when he slowed the stream a bit more. They noted down all they saw, even descriptions of any images which weren't clear and didn't make sense.

"This is incredible, but we must keep it to ourselves. It seems from the witness that the car was deliberately trying to run him down - attempted murder no less!" said Mark full to the brim with enthusiasm. "We must run through *all* the data to see if he remembers that!"

"But that could take weeks or even months at this rate. We can't spend all our spare time staring at that screen. Be realistic Mark," she said irritably. "I know it's fantastic and all that, but can't we leave it at that. This work could already make you famous!"

Mark was pacing.

"But don't you see, we might discover why he was run down. It must be all there in his head. We've just got to hope that he dreamt about it - that is if he remembers it. We must find out," Mark stated emphatically.

Hours of data runs seemed to repeat the same sort of images of movement seen through a train window. They were sure it must have been a train and not a car because no road scenes appeared - no other cars or lorries - just trees and the odd building. Thinking about what things one would see on a train journey convinced them that the flashes of what could only be described as buildings, were in fact the stations, shown for a moment as the train rushed past. Slowing the stream even more didn't help at all, just fuzzy blocks with no detail, just as it would have appeared to him through the window.

"Why do you think there's so much remembered about a train journey? Unless it was a very *long* journey." Mark shook his head, puzzled.

"That's it!" Jane said wide-eyed.

"That's what?"

"It probably *was* a long train journey and this particular dream recording was his mind trying to relive it. It could infer that it was very important to him and that's why he dwelt on it so long. It might not even have been a long trip but just that his mind kept going over and over the same shorter journey, though it's hard to tell," expounded Jane.

"Ah! But there wasn't all that much repetition of individual images or the stations, if they were stations, they all appeared a bit different. I put my money on it being a long journey," he said, looking as if he was glad he'd come to some conclusion after hours of boring viewing.

The data they had run through had been just one REM sleep dream sequence - there were dozens more. The novelty had worn off, and the lack of detail made it seem hardly worthwhile carrying on. Nevertheless they did spend the next three evenings and a whole coinciding day-off plodding relentlessly through the next batch of indistinct images.

It paid off. Towards the middle of the third run a mix of unintelligible images suddenly changed as if the patient had jolted his mind to think of something different. Although the scenes were equally unclear, what this dream showed was very mystifying. Mark and Jane gathered up any enthusiasm they had left and watched a darkened screen with a brighter area jumping around in the middle. What could it be? They watched the images appear for a few minutes and then they changed again as suddenly as before. This time they were witnessing a clear picture of people, lots of people, apparently moving backwards and forwards around the man's field of vision in his mind's eye. It was infuriatingly impossible to make out any facial details, but people they certainly were, the first images which were revealing the undeniable vision of recognisable objects.

This improvement in clarity spurred Mark on to thinking if it was possible to further improve the quality of the images. His equipment wouldn't improve them because that was how they appeared to the victim in his jumbled mind. After all, he was being kept alive by the machines he was plugged into - it was amazing he was able to think or dream anything!

During his time at Addenbrooke's, Mark discovered that a college friend of his was working in the pharmaceutical research department on the far side of the site, and they met now and again to discuss each others work. He only told Pete Glenden about the general work he had undertaken in neurology, much of it to do with some of the other patients he was monitoring, with little mention of the unknown man.

The Summerhouse Project

Pete was employed by the MRC to research into various drugs which could prove useful for the treatment of patients. At the moment he was working on a drug complex which could be used to heighten a patient's morale, one which affected the part of the brain responsible for alertness to artificially block feelings of despondency and apathy, whilst at the same time stimulating the senses. It was a common condition in long term patients who gradually become lethargic and torpid.

Mark was interested in this type of drug being available for those suffering from brain damage in the hope that stimulation may bring about brain cell regrowth and reorganization which might carry on naturally in the brain when the drug was withdrawn. It was one of the many things he and Bruensen discussed at their once-a-week meetings. Pure electrical treatment was also a relevant area for discussion, being used by doctors in cases of deep depression, although it was being phased out in recent years partly for ethical reasons. The drug, in one form, had already gone through clinical trials and was beginning to be used for those patients who would most benefit, particularly those who were inclined to thoughts of suicide. The version Pete was presently involved with was essentially the same chemical complex but had another chemical group attached to the original molecule which it was hoped would further enhance the beneficial qualities of the drug and reduce some of the inevitable side-effects, one of which was loss of appetite.

At his next meeting with Dr. Bruensen, Mark suggested a series of trials of the drug on his patient, as the results may well prove interesting at the very least. Much to Mark's surprise he agreed, as the man's state was considered hopeless anyway. Anything which may result in the patient's recovery to *any* degree would be appropriate, he said, and since the drug was already being introduced in other areas of medicine, he could see no reason against it.

Mark's chemist friend supplied him with the latest drug - the improved version. He had not told Pete why he wanted the so-far untested version of the drug, only that it would be a good opportunity to try it out. The final go-ahead to use the drug was given by Dr. Bruensen's superior. The next day this was done intravenously.

Mark's plan was taking shape, although Jane had gross misgivings about the whole thing. It appeared to her that things were turning in a sinister direction and that Mark had become unreasonably obsessed. As she pointed out to him, his great discovery obtained only by modification of the existing monitoring system was virtually above-board, although he should, strictly speaking, have told Bruensen of his plans. But, he now stood a good chance of ruining his career and his good name, as well as putting his golden discovery in the shade, that is if he chose to reveal it at all!

The Summerhouse Project

CHAPTER SEVEN

THE VISITOR

Mark was determined to go ahead with his plan to gather more REM sleep data whilst his comatose patient was under the influence of the new drug. Jane didn't say anything about their now strained relationship, but she felt that he was so taken up by this project that she was only second best to him. As the week came and went, their hours clashed almost audibly with little time together. The late evenings when they were both at the flat meant little to Jane as it was usually spent with Mark totally engrossed in his work on the new data and her stuck in front of the TV in the bedroom away from his swearing and mutterings when things didn't go quite right for him; he was fast becoming a different person to her now.

Mark had managed to record several sessions of REM sleep data which certainly showed an increase in brain activity under the influence of the drug; the all important sub-modulation waveforms were proportionately larger and more detailed, as he had hoped. On the Friday evening he was all plugged in and ready to go with the first of the new batch of data. Jane had to work late that night so he was on his own without having to worry about Jane's boredom. He was well aware of the problems he was causing with his obsession but he just couldn't help it - he had to see it through now. There were too many unanswered questions arising which he hoped would be partially resolved over the weekend.

The first of the new data was switched through. The monitor flickered into life, and there, as clear as he could have hoped for, was a building he immediately recognised as the Kremlin. Mark was stunned, he knew it was the genuine article. He started a new page in the notebook and jotted down the details. The image came and went a few times before completely fading from view. It was replaced by the face of a woman which also remained on the screen for some time.

At this stage he set the video recorder to record the scenes appearing on the monitor. He again ran the EEG data to capture the view of the Kremlin and then the mysterious face. It seemed to be that of a woman in her late twenties or early thirties, it was difficult to tell, but certainly a very distinctive and attractive young woman. Mark just couldn't come to terms with the fact that he had actually been able to capture clear personal dreams and recollections - images and memories.

He thought over the implications of this. It could be used by the police to discover the truth about a person's criminality. It would doubtless show the crime, if there had been one committed, because it would be the main overriding thing on the suspect's mind. In an unconscious state, control of what was dreamt would be impossible. His invention could also have many other uses, mainly of a sinister nature. He thought deeply about this problem. He could prevent this dream-machine getting into the wrong hands by simply never telling anyone about it and by destroying the evidence. Only Jane knew; could he trust her if it came to it?

His preoccupation with the ethics of the device had taken his mind off the monitor which was still running through the data. When he regained his focus on the screen he just caught a glimpse of a different part of the dream sequence. He re-ran the stream. The face was the last thing he remembered seeing, but now on the screen was a shocking run of images. It started with lots of flashes of different images far too quick to comprehend, but that didn't matter, he could always slow it later on if necessary.

The screen then became dominated by a large black object moving at speed and quickly filling the screen, in fact, the man's mind's eye. This had to be the moment he was run down by the car. The screen image flickered again and returned to the face of the woman. Mark hastily noted down all he saw, even though it was video recorded twice already! The screen then went blank with repeated fuzzy areas and remained so for a long period. It must have been the end of that dream period,

Mark reasoned. He re-ran a previously viewed data set, which as far as he remembered held two REM dreams.

Mark wasn't expecting to see a luggage trunk on the screen, but there it was, plain to see. Why should he be dreaming of a trunk just sitting there? The picture went dark and then repeated a sequence he had seen before on this earlier batch. In the darkness of the image a bright area was moving about all over the place, just as before, but this time with the heightening effect of the drug, the picture quality was enhanced enough for Mark to make out some sort of piping in the bright areas. The bright areas in the surrounding darkness convinced Mark that he was seeing a torchlight beam moving around in the darkness.

Mark re-ran the sequence again. The guy was in some sort of dark tunnel, it was clear to him now. The tunnel had pipes on the walls as tunnels often do - like service tunnels. These image sequences were certainly part of some giant jigsaw puzzle if ever there was. The light continued to move about the screen and then faded. The woman's face reappeared for an instant, but although it was a quick view it was incredibly clear, the clearest image he had yet seen; it was such a beautiful face, somehow hauntingly beautiful. The other REM data sequence was wildly erratic with not one clear image.

Hours had past, Jane would be in any minute now. He felt guilty and went to the kitchen to make coffee for when she arrived. Jane burst into the flat breathless.

"You'll never guess what happened tonight!"

"But are *you* all right? Whatever's happened? Here have some coffee and tell me," Mark said, extremely concerned.

"Your patient in the neurology ward Mark, he's dead, he's really dead!" She gulped down some of the coffee. "No one's sure what happened. He was routinely checked only a few minutes before and then the alarm tone sounded and everyone rushed in."

Mark slumped into a chair, hardly able to believe that the still unknown man was dead.

"Now we'll never know who he was," uttered Mark glumly.

"Oh yes! He had a relative who visited him quite often I understand."

Mark jumped to his feet.

"Oh no he didn't, I would have known about it," he said adamantly. "There was no one!"

"Well, it was awful. This relative was there when it happened. He was in a terrible state, sitting in the corner armchair. He had to be helped out, the poor man was in tears. He must have been very close to him."

"This is not true! No-one *ever* came to see him, he was unknown. We would have known from this so-called relative who he was wouldn't we, in that case," he said, pacing again.

"Yes, of course, I hadn't thought of that. But then I only heard about it this evening from the staff nurse." She finished up her coffee while Mark's cup was forgotten about.

"I know the staff nurse, she would have told me, or someone - anyone - because we desperately needed to know who he was," Mark shouted angrily.

"It's no use getting on at me about it. I'm sick of the whole bloody thing," she said tearfully. Mark comforted her.

"I'm sorry love, I didn't mean to shout at you. It's just that I don't know what's happening - it's so weird and getting weirder I can tell you. We'll get to bed now after a bite to eat and I'll show you some very odd video recordings tomorrow. It *is* Saturday tomorrow . . . isn't it?" he prayed for a 'yes'.

"Yes it is, and I'll get you breakfast in bed. You look really rough Mark," she said sympathetically.

"It should be *me* getting *you* breakfast. I've not been very good to you over the last few weeks. I'll make it up to you as soon as I've sorted out this mess - you see!"

The next day they laid in until lunchtime and had a well earned rest. He showed her the video of the data and she was as stunned as he was at the detail of this batch. Mark switched everything off, saying to hell with it until Monday. This weekend was to be the first time in a long time that they'd spent together away from 'The Machine' as Jane called it.

The weather was glorious, as if someone had planned it to be that way. Mark took her to Grantchester meadows for a good old-fashioned picnic, complete with a giant wicker hamper on wheels. He had emptied a load of wires and gadgets onto the floor, saying that a picnic basket it was, so it's going on a picnic!

The Summerhouse Project

CHAPTER EIGHT

REVELATION

First thing Monday morning Mark called in at staff nurse Hanson's office. She was sitting at her desk behind a large pile of papers.

"My patient died Friday evening I hear!"

"I'm afraid so," she answered matter-of-factly.

This annoyed him.

"What's this I also hear about some relative or other visiting him, who was there when he died?" he said accusingly, feeling the anger well up in to a knot in his chest.

"Yes, your information is quite correct. Where did you hear all this news then?" she questioned sarcastically.

"Is it strange for me to ask about it then, Miss Hanson? He was not only my patient but also my research work! I'm suspicious of his visitor, you know, the one who visits him regularly! He just doesn't fit in does he? Why did you tell Jane he was often here, yet I know nothing of it?"

"Oh I see! This Jane, was it, told you all this," she

retorted.

"And why the hell shouldn't she?" Mark felt himself about to explode with anger.

"Simply, Mr. James . . ."

"*Doctor* James if you don't mind," he cut in.

"Simply, because this Jane is not assigned to this ward at her present stage," she replied drily. "She had no right to be in here!"

Mark was amazed at her attitude; she'd quite obviously heard on the gossip grapevine that they were living together. There were quite a few rather odd middle-aged spinster-types who worked at the hospital living nearby.

"She had a perfect right to be here! We are both involved in research work on this patient. Jane helps me with all the paperwork and number crunching as well as her nursing career to cope with, so I'll thank you to mind your own business Miss Hanson. Got it!" He felt much better after that.

"Now, back to the business in hand," he resumed. "Why do you say he was visited often by this relative, when I, nor anyone else, have ever seen them or been told about them? The police are wanting any information on this mystery patient, so isn't it rather obvious that if this visitor does exist they would undoubtedly know who the patient was?"

It transpired that Miss Hanson, staff nurse, had only ever seen the male visitor on that one occasion and that he had approached one of the sisters on duty that evening saying he was a relative who visited two or three times a week. The sister concerned had only moved to neurology on the Wednesday of that week and automatically took the visitor's word for it and took him to the room. Miss Hanson had only been *told* he had visited other times before by this sister and had no reason to check it out. She did not actually *know* he was a relative at all.

Mark discovered the visitor was helped downstairs, apparently with his hands over his face and sobbing, and was never seen again. Why did no one think to question him about the identity of the victim? It was a missed golden opportunity. Unbelievable! Mark thought the whole thing to be definitely rather on the sinister side. It was virtually known to be a case of attempted murder by hit-and-run.

The question uppermost in Mark's mind was the distinct possibility that the visitor called to finish him off when the car failed to do the job? But if he did murder the unknown victim, how did he manage it in the short space of time between the routine check and the alarm sounding only a few minutes later?

Further investigation revealed the truth. At the time, the patient was being intravenously fed by a drip bottle and tube and a small puncture mark was later discovered in the plastic feeding tube. The autopsy revealed barbiturate in his blood stream.

The police had questioned everybody concerned, including the sister and Miss Hanson. The only way for further investigation was Mark's videos and masses of EEG data yet to be run. He had to find the truth behind this bizarre affair.

*   *   *

Mark and Jane's relationship improved dramatically over the next few weeks and they decided to go out whenever they could and really enjoy themselves. The dream-machine gathered dust, but the remaining data was still going to be looked at when they felt able to face it all again, but the most important thing was Mark's promise to Jane not to become obsessed with it again. The next data run was streamed into the machine a month later. Jane and Mark were now closer than they had ever been.

This next batch was difficult to interpret. It showed the window frame which had been seen many times before, but this time it appeared strangely different. The frame was not entirely clear this time despite the drug enhancement, and the space it enclosed was virtually blank. Every now and again, a solid line came up into the bottom of the frame and went down again, sometimes at an angle relative to the frame's bottom edge. Mark thought back to the train journey sequence with the trees and stations moving past at some considerable speed which had to be slowed down for him to realise what he was actually seeing. But this window frame sequence was entirely baffling.

The Summerhouse Project

Why was there no view out of the window, if indeed it was a window this time. The solid slow-moving part at the bottom sometimes remained hovering as if a plank of wood was being held horizontally and slowly moved about. It would even move up nearly to the top of the frame blocking the otherwise bright area within the frame. If only he could have produced coloured pictures, it would have made the task of interpretation so much easier, or would it?

He thought about it and came to the conclusion that there would quite likely be problems arise with a coloured image. If a person does dream in colour there would have been tremendous technical problems to overcome in extracting that amount of information from the EEG trace signal. Colours would tend to bleed into one another causing false colour images of reduced clarity and definition. He considered that with everything taken into account he was, in fact, better off with black, white and the tonal greys in-between as resolution is far better with a monochrome system.

His mind flipped back to the analogy of a plank being held horizontally, wobbling about at the bottom of the screen. That was it! Horizontal . . . horizon - the horizon, that was what it was - a moving horizon of a flat area of land or sea. Mark's overworked brain went into a higher gear. If it was the sea, he most probably was viewing it from a plane window, as that would also explain the indistinct window frame. The character of the dream, involving two different types of window - the train carriage and the aeroplane windows - disallowed a distinct window frame image of the plane to form in his brain as it continually changed from a rectangle to the roundish type window of an aeroplane. The resultant image was then a mental mix of the two types of window frame his recent memory had in its store, and so appeared in the dream as a blurred frame.

Gradually the jigsaw of important images were accumulating on videotape and described in the note book, but also, and more importantly, the images had been identified. But the images Mark witnessed on one particular run made his senses reel. He would never forget them and they would continue to haunt him for the rest of his days. There, on the screen in front of him was the chilling image of an atomic explosion. It remained on the screen for what seemed like an eternity, gradually changing the shape of its hideous up-welling mushroom cloud. This image was then replaced by the trunk image several times together with flash-frames of numbers.

Mark sat rooted to his chair, unable to come to terms with the scene before him.

"Where had this guy witnessed such a scene? Could he be remembering a film of an explosion? But why had this awful image suddenly appeared to him and how was it relevant to the previous images? Perhaps it was a personal nightmare which just popped into his head. It all seems very strange indeed, trying to piece together these different images." Mark muttered his thoughts.

"Perhaps the trunk blew-up," suggested Jane.

"Good God! Perhaps that's it!" shouted Mark.

"Come on! That's a bit far fetched isn't it? I was only joking!"

"You know how the saying goes: 'Many a true word spoken in jest'. OK Jane. Let's just suppose for a moment that your idea is correct: that the trunk *did* contain a nuclear bomb. Why and where would it be detonated?" questioned Mark, slumping down into his seat awaiting some sort of instant explanation. He was surprised to receive one.

"That's easy - it's obvious isn't it?"

"Is it?" replied Mark tersely. "How do you work that one out then?"

Jane sat at the table with her face squashed up in her palms looking intensely thoughtful.

"Well! The trunk appeared on the screen after the explosion - it sort of ties the two images together somehow - and the numbers!" she said excitedly. "Yes, that's it . . . the numbers. You said they only appeared for a brief moment didn't you? They could represent the settings on the bomb's instrument panel.

"We are only seeing the image in the man's mind as he generated it and not necessarily as it actually was. I think that the numbers only appeared very briefly in his mind because he dreaded them and didn't want to associate them clearly with the actual bomb in the trunk because he knew he had to eventually arm the device. And the bomb, Mark, is somewhere in the Kremlin - in a service tunnel - remember the pipes we saw in the torchlight?"

Mark agreed the visual evidence was convincing.

"But couldn't the whole dream sequence be a fantasy in his head that didn't actually happen at all?"

Jane had to agree that this could indeed be the truth.

"How can we know the truth from fiction? If it *is* the truth, we ought to tell the authorities don't you think?" she reasoned.

Mark looked decidedly worried.

"But who would believe us? And even if we *were* believed and had shown the evidence we have obtained from the dream recorder to the authorities, it could cause an international incident with us stuck in the middle of it all. Perhaps it would be a wise move to leave it all well alone and destroy all the machines and tapes. I tell you Jane, it would make me feel a whole lot better. Besides, we have a future ahead of us, our careers and our love for each other. All that would change if any of this bizarre business became known. We might be in danger because this chap was obviously up to no good and was eventually murdered! He was a secret agent of some sort on this terrible mission; that is if all this stuff is telling us the truth!"

He waved his arm over in the direction of his months of hard work: the hardware he had constructed in the wild hope that he might achieve what was thought unattainable. He was successful, but at what cost?

Mark and Jane agonised over what to do. Days later they came to a decision. The EEG REM data had revealed what could be a terrible truth, one which would have a devastating effect threatening world peace. They couldn't ignore this awful responsibility which now weighed heavily upon their shoulders.

"Are you sure we're doing the right thing Mark?"

"What else can we do? We've said we can't sit back and ignore it!" Mark was showing signs of irritability, obviously caused by the stress they were both enduring, together with their demanding careers which could very soon be threatened, and their own relationship which was too good to destroy.

"Anyway, where would we go to reveal all this secret information?" remarked Jane.

"I'd been thinking about that one. There's really only one person I could go to . . . Bruensen. For one thing he's my boss and I really should have told him about my work on the device from the beginning. He might find out about it all anyway and I need to be the first to tell him; after all it is a medical breakthrough which would boost my career prospects *and* Bruensen's no end. Yes, I must tell old Bruensen. He won't believe a single word of it!"

A smile broke out across Mark's face as he said it, the first Jane had seen for some time. It was as though Mark had suddenly relaxed now he had come to a decision at long last.

The Summerhouse Project

After Dr. Bruensen's weekly get-together to discuss the various patients' progress reports with the staff, Mark took him to one side to ask him if they could discuss some important aspect of his neurological research work.

"Certainly, my boy! When would be convenient?"

"Well, could I speak with you right away - it is rather important." Mark said with a hint of urgency in his voice.

"Fine, fine. Shall we go to my room or yours?" he asked, waving his arms about gesticulating this way or that.

"Yours, if that's OK."

They made off in the direction of Bruensen's room on the floor above.

"Do have a seat, make yourself comfortable. Well, what have you been up to?"

That phrase slightly unnerved him and he sat forward on the edge of the brown leather chair.

"It's to do with my research project on the mystery patient."

"Oh! Yes, a strange business that. It's rather messed up your work to say the least, we'll never know who he was now I imagine!"

"That's the point, we may be able to find out through the work I've been doing," said Mark enthusiastically.

"Your not telling me you got him to talk!" joked Bruensen.

"No, he's been comatose throughout," insisted Mark.

The Summerhouse Project

Mark waded into the complete story, with Dr. Bruensen himself now on the edge of his seat wearing an expression that's hard to describe - a sort of mixture of wide-eyed disbelief and riveting attention. He listened to all Mark had to say without uttering a single word. Beads of sweat had gathered on Mark's hairline making him feel more uncomfortable than he was already, anticipating Bruensen's reaction to what must have sounded like the science-fiction ramblings of a madman.

"I've got to believe you haven't I?" he finally found the words to say.

"Well yes, you have; I've all the proof back at my flat. I really would appreciate it if you could come over and see it all for yourself," he said, half expecting his boss to burst out laughing at such a ludicrous story.

"Keep me away. You are sure this isn't an enormous practical joke that I'm falling for. I mean, it isn't something you've cooked up for rag-week at your old college is it?"

"I only wish it was Dr. Bruensen, I only wish it was as simple and light-hearted as that."

Mark's eyes lost contact with his and he stared at the floor, relieved that at last he had told someone who was prepared to believe him. Bruensen stood up abruptly and he moved across to the window staring out across the open countryside, his eyes briefly followed the Cambridge to London train in the middle distance. Without turning he spoke with a serious tone.

"How many other people know about this?"

"Only one, my girlfriend who is a nurse here. In fact I don't think I could have managed it without her help. She wouldn't have told anyone; it was an obvious understanding between us, especially so because of the nature of the material."

"Quite so, quite so," he repeated. "Right then. You're not the sort of fellow who would make up such a story and then to tell it to your superior; it would completely damage you're credibility as a doctor. Indeed, I must say I have been altogether an admirer of your work here. New ideas and the ability to see them through is what is needed to progress in medical science, but I must say you've certainly surpassed yourself with this one!"

They shook hands and arranged to meet at Mark's flat that evening.

CHAPTER NINE

DR. DAVENPORT

On the way down to his room, Mark's only thoughts were to contact Jane as soon as possible to tell her how it all went and that his boss was coming over that very evening. He found her in the ENT department where she had moved on to as part of her over-all training. She was grabbing a hurried cup of coffee in the staff room before her next port-of-call in another part of the building.

"Another minute and you would have missed me," she said between noisy slurps.

"Listen. I've told old Bruensen everything and how you've helped me, and he's coming over this evening. How are you fixed?"

Jane looked over her shoulder to see if the rest of her team had moved on.

"I'm on until nine tonight, but there is a chance I may get away early. Look, sorry Mark, I really must rush. I'll see you this evening. All right?"

Mark returned to his lab, sat down, and reflected on

the conversation with his boss, trying to recall every word which was spoken to finally convince himself that he'd done the right thing. Deep in thought, the jangle of the telephone returned his mind abruptly to the present. Grabbing the handset he automatically announced himself.

"Hello. James here!" It was Bruensen.

"Mark. I've just been in contact with a good friend of mine; he works at the ministry. He's in the same line of research as yourself, but more in the psychology field. I hope you don't mind, but I invited him to our little get-together this evening. He's really most interested. You should get on well with him."

Mark was furious. In utter disbelief that after all they had spoken of less than half-an-hour ago, there was Bruensen shouting it from the rooftops. It was something he took mistakenly for granted that their conversation was in total confidence and within minutes there he was telling someone else. He couldn't hide his anger and after a lengthy silence he answered Bruensen.

"Look, I'm terribly sorry, but this thing was just between you and me. I just don't want anyone else involved at this stage; I thought you realised the importance of that. You will, with respect, cancel this friend of yours with a suitable excuse; I won't have others involved. I'm sorry but that's how it must be."

The anger and desperate disappointment in Mark's tone came across the phone line loud and clear.

"I'll remind you James, that you work in this

establishment for *me*. The research you've done is a part of the whole department's work and not your personal property. I commend you for this effort which I hope to see the results of this evening - with your permission that is! I will do as you ask and come alone."

Mark calmed his voice as best he could, but could not stop himself shaking inside.

"Please, if you would. This is very important to me, and ninety percent of this project has been undertaken in my own time, in my own flat; that to me, makes it my personal work. I'm sorry if you just don't see it that way, but that's how it is and that's how it'll stay. I hope you will appreciate that tonight. Goodbye."

Mark stopped himself from slamming down the phone - only just, as his finger stabbed at the rest button, *then* he slammed it down, fury having taken a hold of his senses. It was Bruensen himself who asked if anyone else knew about this work and then sets about inviting his friend to his flat!

*   *   *

The evening arrived all too quickly and at just after seven the bell sounded in the kitchen. With a mouth-full of sandwich he answered the door to Bruensen, his shiny silver BMW looking totally out of place in push-bike bed-sit land.

"Do come in."

Bruensen stepped into the small hall area as Mark

closed the door behind him and leant upon it still clutching the old-fashioned brass knob.

"Look, I'm sorry I was somewhat rude on the phone, but really, this thing is bigger than both of us," Mark said firmly.

"I do hope this gadgetry of yours lives up to your vivid description of it."

A half smile formed on his lips, but his eyes didn't respond. It was always an annoying feature of Bruensen: you could never be sure of his mood or what he might be thinking. It was definitely a result of his fixed eyes never changing, even when you think he's making a joke.

The machines were switched on and Mark explained each function along the way. He first showed him how the EEG readings were digitised to be introduced to the computer, and Mark's program forming the video signal necessary to be fed to the monitor. Mark then ran a series of video recordings he'd made of the important scenes - the ones which took days and even weeks to locate as clear as possible to make visual sense.

Bruensen was staggered. He just couldn't believe what he was seeing. Mark proved to him their authenticity by going right back to a particular scene shown to be faithfully extracted from an original EEG trace recording and on through the chain of devices, including Mark's control device he used to slow down the rushes of images generated in the patient's brain. The final set of video recordings told the chilling story clear enough to convince anyone - even Bruensen.

"Of course, you realise what all this means don't you Mark?" He spoke as if he had been consulted for a decision on 'what it all meant'. Mark, more than any of them knew very well what it meant.

"Of course," answered Mark. "The great problem arising is what to do with the knowledge and awesome content of this man's dreams and thoughts. This prototype experiment has been conducted on a far from ordinary person. He was murdered for what he knew, which is now what *we* know! The big question is whether the dreams of this man can be relied upon as fact. I am in no doubt that they *are* the true events in this man's recent past.

"We know from the witnesses report of the accident and from the injuries he received, that he all but survived a hit-and-run assassination attempt. He goes over and over those few moments exactly as they were reported to have happened. I have this event repeated many times in the EEG data streams and recorded onto videotape and still have many more REM data recordings to go through, and there's a strong possibility that new and different images remain to be seen.

"The point is, Dr. Bruensen, that if the car assassination attempt has remained clear in his mind, then it's fair to say that the other events in his mind's eye are just as likely to be based on actual factual events. So there is every reason to believe that he *did* plant a bomb under the Kremlin."

His boss sat there without a word.

"Well, what do you think? Are you as convinced as we are?" Mark said as he turned his ear towards the door. "It's Jane, she had to work late this evening."

Mark opened the door and there stood Jane, dripping wet from a sudden downpour. What he didn't expect to see was a man, who, after shaking his umbrella, proceeded up the steps behind Jane. They appeared to have arrived together.

"Jane, who is this guy with you?" he demanded. Jane looked startled at Mark's response.

"He's a friend of Dr. Bruensen, a Dr. Davenport I think you said didn't you?" She turned to him for acknowledgement.

"Yes, that's right. I only hope you will understand why I had to see you as soon as possible this evening, while Dr. Bruensen was present."

He was a diminutive figure of a man, sniffing because of the rain and fumbling for a handkerchief. Mark turned on Bruensen who had come up behind him.

"I told you *no-one else*. What is this? Who the hell can I trust?" He ushered Jane into the room and gestured for Bruensen and his snivelling sidekick to leave.

"You simply must listen to what Dr. Davenport has to say," Bruensen blurted.

"Clear off, both of you. This isn't a bloody open house you know!"

Bruensen pulled his friend in out of the rain, sending Mark off balance and into the wall.

"You've gone too far this time!" He was about to pull a punch at one of them when Jane took hold of his arm. She yelled at him.

"Mark, Mark . . . listen to me for a minute please. It's OK, really it is."

"How can all this be *OK*?"

"I've just about had enough!" Jane shouted at him to stop and listen to what Davenport had to say before anything else. Reluctantly, Mark went into the room followed by Jane with an arm on his shoulder. The other two men exchanged glances and then looked over towards Mark and Jane. It was Bruensen who broke the tense silence.

"Mark. It was my idea that Dr. Davenport here should approach Jane, underhand as it may seem. He has explained the reason for insisting on speaking to you about your revelations and Jane is in full agreement."

Mark slumped down hard into an armchair.

"All right then . . . fire away, but it had better be good I'm warning you!"

The others sat down while Jane perched on the arm of Mark's chair as if to reassure him that everything was all right. What was to follow, Mark certainly needed to know. Davenport told them that everything they had found out about the patient was true. In fact it was the most remarkable piece of detective work that he had ever heard of, especially by devising such a machine as a dream recorder - a means by which the thoughts and dreams of anyone were there for the taking.

The Summerhouse Project

He was able to tell them the patient's name: Nathan Frazer, an MI5 secret agent no less. Mark's jaw visibly dropped as Davenport continued his story:

Frazer had been highly trained to carry out this mission, one which had been cooked-up by British and US military intelligence. He had entered the Soviet Union as a visitor, and by careful planning by military strategists and Russian associates was able to gain access to the underground conduit system of the Kremlin - the system laid out for the purpose of servicing the piping and cable inputs and outputs of the complex.

He had successfully placed a trunk-sized A-bomb in the very bowels of the communist regime's centre of operations. A high-gain antenna was attached to the case by a cable, to receive and deliver coded signals from a satellite should the need arise. Davenport went on to say that once Frazer was back in England he was to immediately travel to Cambridge to make contact with another agent for the purpose of debriefing. He was never meant to reach the debriefing agent: it was planned to kill him so he could never reveal the purpose of his mission to anyone. Enter Mark.

Then Davenport came to the point.

"You are in grave danger, both of you," he warned, turning to nod at Jane. "These people are ruthless to completely obliterate any evidence whatsoever. As you have seen, they finally got to Frazer - they had to. If this mission and its purpose was ever to leak to the Soviets, just think what it would mean in terms of world security. I personally consider this to be the ultimate act of gross stupidity, which would take the cold war to the very brink of credibility, and an actual declaration of war against this country and the USA."

Dr. Davenport finally located his handkerchief from his soggy mackintosh pocket and proceeded to mop his forehead and neck - not rainwater, but a profusion of sweat which had gradually formed rivulets down his cheeks. It was now glaringly obvious why the two men had to talk to Mark, and he felt bad about his earlier behaviour, which at the time, was entirely understandable. He apologised to them for this, which was anticipated to be a natural response on his part to protect the evidence he had accrued. Mark now had even more reason to keep this awful nightmare situation under control. No-one must find out this information outside of Western military intelligence.

The time had come for Mark to seek advice about what he should do with the tapes, now he knew that what they had revealed to him was solid, horrifying fact. There was no way Davenport could have known beforehand the exact details of the tapes. Then it occurred to him: How *did* this Davenport know the complete details of such a secret plan? Surely he must be in grave danger of the terminal type as well as himself. More so in fact, because he obviously knew about it well before Mark stumbled upon it! He had to ask Davenport how he knew. Mark pulled himself up out of the armchair and looked Dr. Davenport straight in the eyes.

"I've got to know how you came across this information?" demanded Mark. Jane nodded.

Davenport stood up and struggled to remove his mackintosh. Jane helped him and took it into the kitchen. Everyone present had settled down into a sort of all-in-the-same-boat situation. Jane called from the kitchen to ask if anyone wanted tea as she lit the gas under the kettle - it was a welcome break for all of them.

"Dr. Bruensen and myself," began Davenport, "have known each other for a long time. Before he came to your hospital as head of neurology and neurosurgery he was a member of our organization. I'm sure he won't mind me telling you that he was involved in research into the psychology of prospective secret agents, those who were to be considered as special agent material, if you follow what I mean. These potential under-cover agents have to be very carefully vetted over a long period of time before they are approached and offered this work. The psychological make-up of such a person is of prime importance, and this was the task Dr. Bruensen had undertaken within our organisation.

"He and a small elite group of medical men had to get under the skin, so to speak, of these people. They trace all activities and political proclivities since their birth - further back than that. Their parents activities and country of origin has to be known for obvious reasons. Even their sexual preferences are scrutinised to avoid the possibility of blackmail. This vetting process can take many years to complete as thoroughly as is absolutely possible, you understand." Mark nodded. "One such person was Nathan Frazer. Before being approached for the job he eventually undertook, he was carefully monitored for seven years until virtually everything was known about him.

"A great deal of this work was done by Dr. Bruensen, until he left the organization four and a half years ago. He was only allowed to move out of his position when it was sure that he would never speak of this work. He knew very well that if he did, he was a dead man; that was an absolute certainty. He also knew it was Frazer in his department's hospital bed - he had recognized him on admission. Dr. Bruensen and I are risking our lives to find a way of saving yours, and that now includes Jane."

Davenport looked over to where she was sipping her tea, his eyes damp with concern for the young couple's safety.

"My God!" exclaimed Mark. "This is not true! It's a bloody nightmare, I'll wake up soon!"

"I'm sorry. I'm so terribly sorry things have turned out like this. Ironically your wonderful invention has turned against you, and now we must make plans to save ourselves," he said, in a shaky voice. "It's not myself I particularly care for, but for you two, who should never have become involved in this awful murderous business, and for Dr. Bruensen. If the car 'accident' had gone successfully to plan, none of this would have happened.

"So you're a member of this organization are you? MI bloody five?" The silence which followed confirmed it. Davenport was quite obviously ashamed of his involvement with this particular department and looked a beaten, broken husk of a man who seemed determined to do something meaningful with his remaining years - or weeks!

"You see, vast sums of money are offered in this business, and it's only when you're older and wiser that you realise the money isn't the important factor. Frazer was offered a phenomenal sum of money, five million I think the figure was, and a place in the sun for the rest of his miserable life. What he didn't know was that he would never live to enjoy it; it was all part of the overall plan, mainly masterminded by the Americans. It wasn't until he had completed the job that the order was made to snuff him out - the poor bastard!"

Davenport was sure spilling the beans, as if he had nothing left to lose.

"The decision to plant the bomb was in case things got out of hand between the two superpowers, allowing Britain and America the upper hand - a sort of trump card which could be played as blackmail."

"One which the Russians couldn't risk calling their bluff," added Mark.

"That's about the long and short of it," Bruensen interjected.

Bruensen and Davenport finally left in the small hours. Bruensen gave his friend a lift, as Davenport had made his way that day by bus and walking from the railway station in the morning. He had boarded the first train from London after receiving Bruensen's telephone call the previous day. The car pulled into the driveway of Bruensen's house in the pretty satellite village of Little Shelford, a short distance from Addenbrooke's. Dr. Davenport was invited to stay overnight before catching the early morning train back to his London flat.

The Summerhouse Project

CHAPTER TEN

ABDUCTION

The next few days seemed like weeks for Mark and Jane. Every spare minute of their time was spent dismantling the machines which had suddenly changed their lives and indeed threatened it. It was true that all they had to go on was the video evidence and the story told by Davenport and supported by Mark's boss, but with all things considered that was more than enough to convince them to act quickly and cover their tracks carefully.

By the end of the following week, all the collected EEG traces and recordings, together with the video cassettes, computer software and hard-drives had been fed well and truly to the hospital's incinerator beneath the towering twin-chimney landmark of Addenbrooke's hospital. All that remained was the device he'd constructed to create the video output to the monitor screen from the EEG tape modulations via his computer program. This was disposed of mainly by use of a sturdy pair of pliers. He tried not to think of the hours he had spent making it, as the pieces dropped into the dustbin.

One thing he was pleased about was that he had a knack of remembering detail, and so he was confident that if and when the time was right he could recreate this transposer-amplifier circuit straight from memory. The other of these two vital components of his dream machine was the computer programme he had spent weeks producing. By the time he had completed it, all the essential details were etched into his brain, never to be forgotten. This ability to memorise quite complex information had been an absolute boon to him at school and then later on at college. He was able to tap into this super-memory at examination times and pour it all out onto the paper in a very short time.

Now, without a trace of evidence remaining, either at the flat or his lab at the hospital, he and Jane began to relax a little. Dr. Bruensen was pleased and he and Mark had many occasions to speak at length about psychology, which was now beginning to interest Mark; they were becoming more like friends than boss and worker. Since that night, they shared a common bond - a bond of fear that the organisation, as they called it, might one day - any day - descend upon them without warning for what they knew. Only time would tell. Mark just couldn't bear the thought of forever looking over his shoulder and not knowing who to trust. This realization hung over Jane and Mark like a great black cloud.

The Summerhouse Project

*   *   *

During one of Bruensen's frequent visits to London hospitals, Davenport arranged to meet for lunch. More details had become available to Davenport in the course of his work. He disclosed to Bruensen that the staff nurse Hanson had been offered a large sum of money to 'pull the plug' on Frazer, but couldn't bring herself to go through with it - that was when the 'visitor' came to sort out the problem. However, what she *was* able to do was to regularly inform her contact of all she knew about the research work being carried out on Frazer by Mark under the supervision of Dr. Bruensen. She knew Mark was collecting data into a recorder of some kind, which he then took away with him. She had secretly observed his activities, and on some occasions had deliberately gone into the room to 'check' the life support system to see if Mark was doing anything of a suspicious nature with the EEG monitors.

She had reported that during these occasions, especially when no-one else was in the room, she had been tempted to go ahead and sabotage the vital umbilicals which were keeping Frazer alive. Bruensen, as an ex-MI5 psychologist was also monitored, being Mark's boss, and naturally thought to be overseeing his research work, although at the time he didn't know of Mark's 'homework'!

Davenport was soon a dead-man. He was discovered by a group of late night revellers hanging by a piano wire beneath London's Southwark bridge. Bruensen was devastated to hear of his friend's death in such a terrible manner. Mark and Jane were fond of the frail old gentleman with such a great concern for their safety without much thought for his own.

Bruensen knew the techniques which would almost certainly have been applied to him in order to get him to reveal other names. He felt sure that he wouldn't have spoken of anybody even under the most intense forms of torture and interrogation. He would have been a true professional to the last.

What would the organization have made of Mark's work on Frazer? Surely there was no way they could have found out about the dream recorder, Hanson couldn't possibly have known anything about that - could she? These and many other thoughts plagued Bruensen as well as Mark and Jane. Things were getting a bit too warm and uncertain.

*   *   *

An evening was set aside for discussion. Jane had prepared a meal and expected Mark and Bruensen to arrive at about eight. Soon the familiar silver BMW came to a halt outside the flat. Jane waved from the net-curtained window and returned to the kitchen for final preparation of their meal. They both arrived in the flat looking pale and concerned - it was Jane who always had a ready smile which was always most welcome. Mark often wondered how much this whole business worried her. He felt angry with himself for ever having involved her in such a problem which she didn't in the least deserve.

"Right then!" Jane said, clapping her hands. "What would you like to drink, Dr. Bruensen?"

"Well, for a start, I would very much appreciate it if you would call me Carl, out of hours that is, and I would like some red wine if you have any. Thank you!"

Jane disappeared into the kitchen, arriving back moments later in a dilemma.

"I don't seem to be able to shift this wretched cork!" groaned Jane, with the bottle between her knees and the embedded corkscrew held firmly in both hands.

"Here, for goodness sake let me at it," insisted Mark. The bottle gave a loud squeak and a resounding pop.

"Mark. What was that?" Jane turned her head.

"What was what Jane?"

"That thump as the cork popped. I think it came from out the front somewhere," insisted Jane. They all moved over to the window, with Carl commenting on how good the dinner smelled, raising his nostrils into the air in an exaggerated fashion.

"It's your car - some silly bugger's hit it!"

"Oh! Christ, No! I've just had a dent in the bumper seen to last week!"

"It's one hell of a lot worse than a bumper I'm afraid."

99

Carl pulled the curtain clear, then leapt to the front door and out into the street, quickly followed by Mark. They knew Bateman street was a bit on the narrow side, but this looked deliberate. Smashed into the rear of Carl's beloved BMW was an old beat-up Capri, but no one was there. Their first thought was that whoever it was had just panicked and ran, but there didn't seem as if there was enough time. There was a person crouched down in the driving seat. Carl peered right into the Capri's open window and found himself looking down the barrel of a shotgun. Neither men moved.

"Is there anybody in there?" questioned a concerned Mark.

Quietly, Carl answered: "Yes . . . there is someone . . . I don't know what to do."

Before anything could be done, another car pulled out of the continuous row of cars lining the street. It screeched to a halt in front of them as the man with the gun sat up and jumped from the Capri.

"Just get in the car," were his only words.

The shotgun was placed over Carl's left ear. Everything had happened so fast - even terrified passers-by seemed to blur, just as if for all the world time had hiccuped on by thirty seconds or less. The two men could do no other than fall into the back seat of the other car. The gunman then slammed his car door with such force that its window shattered and then got in with them. Both Carl and Mark thought it was the shotgun in the confusion and instinctively cowered into the seat.

Jane's scream merged with the scream of tyres on tarmac as the car sped off towards the main road and headed in the direction of Trumpington. Some neighbours rushed into the flat to catch hold of Jane as she slid down the window towards the floor. She sobbed and screamed uncontrollable obscenities.

The Summerhouse Project

CHAPTER ELEVEN

EVIL GRANT

After what seemed like an hour of cramped terror, the car finally stopped at a place neither of them recognised. The driver and the man with the shotgun pulled open both rear doors.

"Come on, out you get!" a voice demanded in a surprisingly educated accent. They half stepped and half rolled out of the car expecting the sound of the end. It didn't come. Instead they were told to walk along a heavily wooded path which curved away in front of them. They quickly exchanged glances, thinking exactly the same thought: If they hadn't been killed by now, then what fate lay ahead?

On they walked until a long low wooden building came into view. It was obvious to them that it was a laboratory of some sort. BOC gas cylinders were neatly stacked against the wall, chained in place. Through the dirty windows they could see familiar apparatus: glassware, plastic tubing, at least two fume cupboards and wooden benches. As they passed each window, it reminded them of their student days slaving over a hot Bunsen. At the end of this long laboratory was a large concrete circle with a post-hole at its centre, rather like a disused playground with the roundabout removed. No one said a word, there was little to say, and little point in trying to strike up any kind of meaningful conversation. It was this realisation of familiar laboratory surroundings which sent shivers down Mark's spine. Carl was expressionless. The hut door swung open as he came face-to-face with a short, stout man wearing a bowler hat. It was now, that Mark let a smirk appear on his face. It was some enormously expensive, elaborate practical joke; it had to be with a funny man in a bowler hat standing there straight-faced. Mark let out a chuckle, he had been under the powerful gripping control of adrenaline for too long - he simply let go at the point where his mind now believed it to be safe.

"Hello Carl." A high pitched voice broke the silence, curling around the 'r' in Carl.

"Hello Grant, long time no see, as they say!" answered Carl as quick as a flash. Mark was in such a strange state of mind by now, believing the situation to be a stupid prank, that he burst out laughing at the little man in the bowler. The man behind him broke Mark's arm in response to a casual nod from the man called Grant. Mark lay on the cold concrete floor with his left arm twisted awkwardly behind him moaning in agony - staring with disbelief.

Again came the odd high voice:

"You're very lucky it wasn't Craig's shotgun - it will take your head clean off your shoulders, Mark the film man."

Mark shuddered, half with the pain and half with the realisation that this fellow Grant knew about the videos. How could he know? Carl must have told them, he convinced himself. Who could he ever trust again? No one else *could* know - only Jane. No. It couldn't be her he thought - but she didn't come out into the street did she? His mind went into a whirl and into blackness.

The man Craig was a tall thin person with a pock-marked face and thin receding dark hair greying at the temples. He always carried his shotgun and looked as if he only needed the smallest of excuses to use it. A surge of cold force brought Mark almost instantly back to reality from his crazy dreaming. Craig stood before him clasping an empty, dripping galvanised pail; he wore the strangest of expressions - a sort of schoolboy delight at being in charge. Mark was tied to a chair with his hands bound tightly behind his back. Pain surged from his broken arm, now grotesquely swollen around his elbow. He sat there cold and wet through, Craig not moving - just staring.

The hut door opened and in walked Grant, still wearing the bowler hat.

"Hello Mark," he said, still curling his tongue around the 'r', "You know, Dr. Bruensen and I have had a nice long chat about you."

"Oh yes!"

105

"Yes we *have*. He's been telling me more about your little invention - you remember - the gadget for dreamers. Do you know . . . at first he would tell me nothing, and so we had to be a little persuasive. Don't you concern yourself about him. You have a job to do here and you will do it!" he warbled confidently. "Untie him. He needs to stretch his legs!"

Grant left the room, leaving Mark with the other man. He swiftly untied him and asked if he could stand.

"Who are you people?" Mark demanded. To his surprise the man answered him.

"It's better you don't know, although you must have some idea." He spoke in a croaky whisper as if he had something wrong with his throat. Mark recognised him as the driver.

"Where are we going?" questioned Mark as he was shown the door.

"Only a short way - to another lab."

Mark carried his left arm in an attempt to ease the pain. Inside the building he was expertly attended to: his arm was held in an adjustable brace to align the broken bone. He then received a pain killing shot in his upper arm.

"You'll feel a lot better after that," the man whispered. He was obviously a trained nurse or doctor, he knew exactly what he was doing.

"What are you doing in a place like this?" asked Mark.

"It's rather a long and complicated story," he said, gesturing for him to lie on the hospital type couch. "Give it about half-an-hour, the pain should go quite a bit by then."

Mark found himself thanking the man who was instrumental in abducting him. He then remembered Bruensen.

"Where is Dr. Bruensen? How is he?" he called out after the man had left the room. After a pause, the man came back into the room.

"Just be thankful you're not in the state he's in."

Mark felt his stomach churn.

"What do you mean? *What* state is he in?" he demanded.

"I'm going to attend to him again now . . . he's alive . . . just, poor devil. Grant eventually got the information he wanted. That's all he cares about - information, and he doesn't care how he gets it either. Believe me I know."

He pointed to his throat briefly and then left the room, leaving Mark alone with his thoughts - terrible thoughts. He must somehow get to see Bruensen.

A numbing thought then sprang up in his confused mind: 'If Bruensen had given Grant the details of his dream recorder, had he also told him that Jane knew about the contents of the tapes?' He then realised that Jane couldn't be the informer, because if she had been, this gang wouldn't have needed him alive to tell them about it; but clearly they did want him alive and he guessed what for!

Grant commanded him to recreate his machine, there in the laboratory. Mark was told that they would supply any piece of equipment he needed. If he refused, then he would suffer pain he couldn't imagine: Davenport and Bruensen were proof enough! There seemed to be no alternative but to comply with Grant's order. He reckoned that during the time necessary to construct the dream recorder he might figure out some sort of plan to escape this nightmare.

Already present in the remarkably equipped laboratory, were two fully functional EEG recorders and all the necessary hard and software - bang up to date stuff - no corners cut. Fully adjustable couches were beside each of the two recorders - but who were going to be the test subjects? Mark listed all the items he would need and incredibly they arrived within the next few days. Mark had no idea where it all came from.

He was well looked after by the man with the whispering, croaky voice - that was obviously his part in this grim affair. He was called by a strange-sounding name by the others, but when Mark asked, he gave his name as Michael. Mark slept in a small but comfortable room just along the narrow corridor from the main lab he was working in. Food and drink was brought to him by Michael. He didn't hear or see anyone else at all once he started on the machine.

Uppermost in his thoughts were Jane and Bruensen; he had no way of finding out about them. Although he couldn't see or hear them, he sensed that others were somewhere in the long, low lab building shrouded by thick woodland in every direction. He reckoned since he was at one end, they were at the other, including Bruensen.

He was about half way through the construction of his EEG to video device one day about a week later, when he saw the others - but no Bruensen. Grant and the gun-toting Craig were moving through the trees and then disappeared from view. About an hour later they returned and made their way towards the other end of the building. Repeated questioning about Bruensen or anything which wasn't to do with the work only produced silence - Michael revealed nothing - he knew his life depended on it.

Mark now had to sit down and remember the computer program which was committed to memory. The task was harder than he had anticipated. The events of the past week or so, and the shock to his system of a broken arm, had sapped not only his physical energy but also his mental ability for recall, which usually came as second nature to him. Many trial and error attempts were run until he eventually came up with the goods. In a way he enjoyed the challenge of recreating his masterpiece purely from memory, but on the other hand, who was the intended victim to be plugged in?

Towards the end of the second week, the bowler-hatted Grant paid him an unexpected visit. He moved quietly to an unnerving position behind him as he was wiring-up the electrodes. Then, in a quiet voice right next to his ear, he began to speak to Mark.

"Everything coming along just fine is it?" Grant's voice impediment irritated Mark to the point of distraction. He could knock the little fellow to the ground with a single blow, but he knew that would be as far as he got with Craig lurking about, besides he'd had enough of broken bones. He turned to answer Grant.

"I think so."

"You must *know* so, Mark! A lot depends on it . . . like your well-being."

Grant tapped a little stick on the bench right next to him - another of this funny little man's props.

"Look, you know all those who found out about the Kremlin bomb, and I suppose you'll kill them all off one by one until your sadistic mind has been sated, so why have you got me here building the wretched machine again?"

There was a nasty silence. Grant had again moved behind him. His stick came down hard on the hand of his broken arm making Mark wince with the sudden pain.

"How dare you speak to me like that. It is your first and last warning."

Grant left the room, leaving behind the sickly odour of some cheap aftershave and sweat. Mark had smelt it before somewhere.

By the middle of the next week the machine was ready. He had serious misgivings about announcing its completion because he didn't know what would happen next. Besides, if he pretended it wasn't ready he could play for more time in the hope that the police or someone would find them. He knew it would be most unlikely as this particular department of MI5 was a law unto itself. This little band of heavies were obviously paid to do the dirty work and get results!

A couple of days later he could stand the suspense no longer; he asked Michael to tell Grant it was ready. A few minutes later, in walked the bowler-hatted wonder. He walked up and down surveying the work.

"Wonderful Mark, I'm so glad you could manage it with that wonderful brain of yours," he remarked sarcastically. "Now, what's next on my list you're wondering. Ah! Yes! Someone to test it all out . . . to see if it works . . . who shall it be?"

He stared hard at Mark as he spoke again.

"It just happens that we have just the fellow!"

He beckoned over to Michael who then left the room, returning with a blanket-covered body on a trolley. Grant produced his little stick and flicked back the sheet to expose the face of an unconscious Bruensen. He'd been treated badly with contusions covering his head. Mark found it difficult to comprehend that anyone could do this to a fellow human being just for what he knew.

"As you can see Mark, dear Dr. Bruensen has not been . . . what shall I say? . . . helpful, and has met with a slight accident."

A sickly smile spread over his face as he tapped the unconscious Bruensen on the head with his stick. Grant was all that was evil rolled into one. Mark had no idea of the damage done to his friend's brain - he could only guess. He was filled with fury and hate for Grant, the adrenaline raced through his body making him shudder.

"You barbaric evil bastard," he shouted at Grant. "There's no way you'll get away with this!"

Mark gave up all fear for his own safety - now things had gone too far. Grant didn't react at all, except for that smile again. He then reached inside his pin-striped jacket pocket and held up a blank card for Mark to see. Grant was loving every minute of his foul ways as he slowly turned the card over to reveal a photograph of Jane. Grant burst into hysterical cackling laughter as he watched the expression on Mark's face change from anger to stark horror at what he saw. Realising he was beaten, his hand hid his eyes as he slumped into the desk chair.

"There. Isn't it amazing what a little photograph can do? So much power Mark, so much power," he gloated looking at the photo himself. "Such a pretty girl . . . if you like that sort of thing."

Mark's voice came quietly from behind his hand.

"What have I got to do for you to leave her alone. She's done nothing!"

"Well, I would have thought that was obvious my boy. Plug him up." He gestured with his eyes towards

Bruensen. "I want to know what he's dreaming about!"

Mark nodded, still with his hand over his face fighting back the waves of emotion which flowed through him: for Bruensen and Davenport, but most of all for the girl he loved and may never see again. Even if she survived it all, he couldn't imagine Grant leaving him alive - he knew far too much.

Mark began the sickening task of wiring up Bruensen to the EEG recorder. This involved fixing small electrodes to the skin in many different places over his head. They were held in place by an electrically conducting sticky gel with the hair carefully parted to facilitate good electrical contact. The many wires were held in place on Bruensen's head by a rubber skull-cap. All was now ready as Grant had wished, even though Mark had no guarantee whatsoever for Jane's safety.

Mark went through the set-up procedure of each instrument in turn until the final stage of tuning in the monitor to the computer containing the loaded programme he had also recalled from memory. Mark sent Michael to ask when Grant wanted him to start recording the dreams. The message came back that he was to call for Grant the moment any images appeared. Bruensen could easily have suffered a great deal of brain damage judging from the kick marks all over his head and neck. He couldn't help thinking that he would have been better off dead; he might survive only to spend the rest of his days in a vegetative state of oblivion.

No REM was evident, which compounded Mark's fear of serious brain damage. Days went by with still no evidence of dreaming taking place. Bruensen was on a nutrient drip-feed system, just as Frazer had been in Mark's own department. He couldn't help wishing that he could return to those happier times. Everything was now in such a terrible mess, through which he could see no way out.

He eventually called for Grant, to tell him that it wasn't going to work, as Bruensen was more dead than alive - no response. Grant was furious, but didn't take his anger out on anyone - he must have known that a beating such as that would not leave much to work on. Carl Bruensen died in the early hours of the following day and was removed from the lab. Mark knew he would be disposed of in some uncaring manner. He wouldn't even have the privilege of attending the funeral of a good and highly thought of friend which he had become. He couldn't help wondering what plans the animal Grant had for him?

He didn't have to wait long to find out. Somehow Grant had been able to procure a medical doctor, who was most probably blackmailed into Grant's service as Mark had been to wire up his friend. This doctor, introduced to Mark as Jim, sat down next to him at his desk and showed him an ampoule containing a solution who's name label Mark immediately recognised - it was the compound given to him by his research chemist friend at the hospital.

"How on earth did you find out about that?" questioned Mark. "That's impossible!"

"I would have thought you'd guess that one," remarked the doctor. "Your Dr. Bruensen did reveal one or two things during his interrogation I'm told. He knew you were using this drug on Frazer and where you obtained it. When I was told to get hold of it from your lab, nothing could have been simpler. A doctor in a white coat breezing into the department to collect some drug or other from the fridge . . . it happens all the time, no-one takes the slightest notice, especially with Bruensen not being about. Incidentally, there's great concern as to where you both disappeared to. Apparently the police have been asking questions in and around the department and the neighbours where you live. I overheard Bruensen's secretary telling it all to another girl . . . "

Mark broke in - excited concern in his eyes.

"Another girl you said . . . What did she look like? . . . Was she quite tall with long black hair?" Mark's heart was pounding in anticipation of his reply.

"No, she definitely wasn't dark; she had one of these short, bleached, spiky haircuts."

Utter disappointment showed on Mark's face.

"Why? Who were you expecting it to be?" Jim shook the small ampoule as he spoke.

"Oh! I just hoped it would be a friend of mine . . . that's all." Mark's voice dropped away to a whisper. "You sound as if you work at Addenbrooke's too," Mark inquired.

"Yes, I do now. What I mean is I've moved here from a Manchester hospital to gain a wider experience; it's a great hospital here in more ways than one. I've had to hurriedly arrange a week off for this little game, and I'd only been there for two weeks, but they didn't seem to mind. Look, I'm really sorry about all this, especially since you're in the same line of business. But I desperately needed the money."

"Yeah! You need the money and I need my life! You do know what's going on here don't you?"

"Well, not really. I wasn't allowed to ask too many questions; just enough to do what I've been paid to do. In fact I don't really want to know too much!"

"Let me tell you a few facts then Jim. This is all secret service stuff we've got ourselves into; you realised that much surely?"

"I sort of guessed it might be something like that," he answered, as if he really *didn't* want to know.

"Incidentally," asked Mark sarcastically, "just what is it you've been paid to do? As if I can't guess!"

"Sorry, but Grant wants *you* wired-up. Bruensen was too far gone as you know."

"What's to stop us walking out of here?" said Mark optimistically. "I hardly see a soul about except for Michael, and I feel sure he'd turn a blind-eye or come with us."

"I wouldn't bank on it. Grant seems to have a hold over all of us. Besides he's got the whole place neatly tied up from the little I've seen of this place!" warned Jim. "Some sort of mirror system linked up to video cameras that look along either side of the building and the ends. Anyway, there's that madman Craig lurking around somewhere - the guy with the shotgun - finger glued to the trigger. It was him and some other guy who brought me here."

Without warning Grant appeared at the door of the lab and sauntered over to where the doctors were sitting.

"No time for talking!"

His appearance and sickly falsetto voice made their skin creep. He turned to Jim.

"Put him under then - what are you waiting for?" Grant then turned towards Mark. "You'll never guess what this gentleman is going to do with you my friend - he's going to hypnotise you!"

Grant gave out a clipped cackle of insane laughter. Jim and Mark exchanged glances.

"You'll never do it!" Mark confidently proclaimed. Mark had little choice but to climb up onto the surgical couch in response to Jim's gesture. He turned down the room lighting and switched on a strobe light, aimed about a foot from Mark's squinting eyes - eyes shut or not made little difference, the light was too intense. Jim adjusted the flashing intervals gradually, until a moment was reached when the frequency of the flashing seemed to coincide and resonate with Mark's natural body frequency. He was then given an injection of the enhancement compound.

"That should do it!" said Jim looking into Grant's evil eyes.

"Interesting . . . very interesting what you medical chappies can do," Grant replied.

Mark shuddered and convulsed violently, then lapsed into unconsciousness. The next thirty minutes or so were spent placing the electrodes over Mark's head and plugging him into the electroencephalogram. The rest of the machine array had remained set up since Bruensen had lain on the same couch Mark now occupied. A serious attempt had been made by Mark to make his mind a blank, although he didn't think for one moment that it would work, especially for someone like himself who had a marvellous memory which would presumably work against his conscious wish to blank out all thoughts. Grant remained in the room as Jim monitored the output on the pen recorder as well as the video screen. The reading showed the characteristic trace of an unconscious person; Jim and Grant had to wait for the REM sleep period to begin.

Both Jim and the odious Grant looked forward to seeing just what Mark's invention was capable of, but for very different reasons: Jim for technical reasons and Grant to obtain the evidence he needed of exactly what Mark knew, if indeed he thought or dreamt of the particular events which were relevant to Grant's expectations. At last, after a long wait mostly in silence as the two men had very little they wished to speak of to one other, Mark's eyes showed movement under the lids. Both turned to watch the screen. An image appeared showing unclear flashes of what appeared to be a speeded-up vision of the construction of electric circuitry. Mark was reliving parts of the complicated construction of his device.

The next sequence of events in Mark's mind were very much clearer. A picnic scene came into view. A girl, Jane, sat amidst a display of food and drink on an enormous table-cloth with clear images of her face appearing intermittently. Grant was beginning to nod off to sleep, perched on the corner of the bench. Jim certainly wouldn't tell him if anything significant came up, and the video recorder wasn't yet running.

Grant suddenly came to his senses as he gradually slipped from the corner of the bench. This joke of a man and his affected mannerisms were amusing to watch, but the humour was soured by his grossly perverted mind and sadistic tendencies. Unfortunately for Jim, Grant sensed his stifled smirk threatening to break out into laughter. With lightning speed he thrashed his stick across Jim's face and droplets of blood formed along the gash dripping onto his white coat.

"You bastard!" he yelled as he left his seat and flew at Grant with his feet leaving the ground. A violent struggle followed as Jim tried to silence the evil Chaplin parody. Grant was held down by the heavily built doctor, crumpling the wretched bowler he always wore. A hideous high-pitched pig-squealing scream left

Grant's mouth before Jim could jam his hand over it.

The door flew open to reveal the equally sadistic Craig complete with his shotgun. The doctor lifted Grant to his feet in one great heave as he screeched out an order for Craig to shoot. Jim knew he would hit Grant as well, so stuck him in the line of fire. Just at that moment Grant pulled his stumpy legs from the floor leaving Jim with his dead-weight he couldn't hold.

As Grant fell to the floor, the surprised doctor saw Craig level his gun at his now unprotected body. But it was Jim's head which burst open in a multicoloured split-second, leaving his body to slump over Grant, spurting blood and brain matter over his upturned bald, bare fat head. At the instant of his death, Jim's head almost sought revenge, blasting its contents onto Grant's face and open mouth.

The tangled bodies lay there. The remains of the doctor pinning the heaving Grant to the swilling floor as he violently vomited in response to the emptying of Jim's neck and head. Craig was loving every second of it. He'd used his shotgun and held an expression of glee as to what the weapon had achieved, turning the weapon over and over in his filthy sweating hands as if admiring its aesthetic qualities.

CHAPTER TWELVE

OVERDOSE

A full hour later and the evil Grant was still heaving onto the grass beside the hut, having managed to persuade Craig and Michael to pull him out from under Jim's twitching body. Not far from the spot where the bodies had vented their contents, the still unconscious and blissfully unaware Mark, lay on his now blood splattered couch, with the monitor still reproducing the thoughts and dreams from within his mind. The cleaned-up shaking Grant was ripe for revenge. He had already given a present to Craig for his accuracy, but sadly not for his timing! He wasn't to be seen for the rest of that day! Poor Michael was ordered to clean away Jim's remains - a task which was nearly impossible to accomplish if it were not for the persuasive endearing nature of Grant.

Grant was determined to carry on with searching through Mark's mind. The ampoule of drug stolen from Mark's lab was a chemical compound called Encephalin B, used in very small amounts on Frazer to stimulate the brain and so enhance awareness. The normal dosage had been carefully worked out during clinical trials at the hospital, and only very small doses were permissible at no more than 0.3 millilitres. Grant didn't know this. He only knew from the dying Bruensen that it had been used with success on Frazer revealing the A-bomb plant. The dispensing ampoule contained a little more than 4 ml. as three doses had been used over a period of time on Frazer. Grant pulled apart the remaining sterile syringe wrapping and broke out its needle from the little orange-coded capsule. Clumsily he fixed on the needle and stuck it into the red rubber seal of the Encephalin B ampoule, filling the 5 ml. syringe with all the remaining drug solution - over thirteen times the safe dose limit. With no preliminary aseptic procedure he pushed the needle into the fattest vein he could find and emptied the syringe. There and then, his twisted mind convinced him that he would make a good doctor.

Mark's body convulsed, proving to Grant that it was working OK. It wasn't. By this time the hypnotic state had worn off and Mark was slowly coming round. Grant didn't know anything about hypnosis and was surprised to see Mark's movements increase. He shot bolt upright and leapt from the trolley couch onto the concrete floor trailing the wires behind him. As he writhed about the electrodes came away from his head taking the rubber skull-cap with them.

Grant watched in amazement as Mark shook and shuddered in response to the overdose of stimulant as the effect of the hypnosis wore off. He was now aware of his state and looked around with staring dry eyes. The fall had shifted his arm brace out of alignment causing him considerable pain. The drug began to run its course taking control of Mark's mind, transforming reality into a state of surrealism.

For once Grant didn't know what to do! He could only see the results of his stupid blunder: Mark writhing and thrashing on the floor. The tremendous overdose was heightening his general awareness out of all proportion. An insidious poison magnifying his sensory perception to levels far beyond his control. Ordinary noises became extraordinary. Deafening torturous sounds assailing his auditory senses, which themselves were becoming increasingly more sensitive - supersensitive. Previously unheard sounds were beginning to filter in, mixing and jangling into unbearable cacophony. Mark was devastated by the onslaught of sounds from the surrounding equipment. High frequencies generated by the fluorescent lights and even his own heartbeat pounding like a demented drum; the rush of blood through his body sounding like a strong wind through tall trees. Hallucinations swamped his mind: grotesque images of things and people he loved and loathed loomed and zoomed over and through him, being part of him then apart from him, or not him at all.

His auditory sense overwhelmed him as it entered the microcosm of atomic structure. He sensed he could hear the electrons struggling their way through the metal conducting crystalline structure of the electrical wiring and on through the circuit boards, audibly suffering to squeeze through resistors and the other components to reach their destinations as fast as they could. Was he really sensing this? Perhaps it was purely the product of an hallucination.

Dare he open his eyes? If that was what he was thinking. Was he able to think? His eyes opened. The room appeared to be slowly pulsating like a camera zoom-in and out, in and out. All he saw was distorted like a Salvador Dali nightmare or a Morits Escher perspective. The room would spin, and then stop. The ceiling low, then so high.

Madness gripped him like a vice. Thoughts of infinity seized his racked senses that remained as sense at all, sending him into cosmic flight - through Death, through Time, through Eternity, and engulfing vortices to Singularity. Mark wrenched himself half up onto a chair. Grant had long gone, terrified out of his wits. Something was changing, he could just sense that. The multidimensional existence he thought he had now become, was fighting, hunting to condense and reunite as four. Was that right? Was that the way things should be? Was there time?

The sweat bubbled through his skin and over him, his hair in dripping rat's tails. He could not see what he should see - perhaps he was dead! 'I'm dead', he thought - if he could think at all. "I'm dead", he said, if he could say at all. Mark finally collapsed, soaked through the skin by his own bodies attempt to flush out the demon drug. He had won - just! Michael had stood in the doorway watching the battle between good and evil. He knew there was nothing he could do; he'd just waited and hoped.

When finally all was peace, he moved over to where Mark lay quietly panting and sobbing in the depths of exhaustion. He reached down to Mark's head and cradled it in his lap, unconsciously stroking away the lank hair. Mark had become like a child in need of reassurance after a nightmare. Michael gave that reassurance, just as he had done many times with his own child.

During the next few hours darkness fell. Both men slept until first light. Mark opened his eyes, looked around and wondered to himself what the hell had happened. He felt as if he'd been kicked senseless as Bruensen had been. He looked down to see Michael and shook him awake.

"What's been going on here Mike? Where's Grant? We must get away from here!"

Michael groaned as he rubbed his eyes awake, blinking into the bright morning light streaming in through the lab window.

"Mark. Are you all right for God's sake? You've been through Hell and out the other side, mate!" he said with a worried expression on his face.

"Well it certainly feels something like that. Tell me what happened?"

"What happened here scared the shit out of Grant. He and Craig left in a mighty hurry late yesterday afternoon – Craig even left his shotgun here, leant up against the fridge!"

Mark was very unsteady on his feet, but made an effort to clear up the mystery of what had happened to make Grant and Co. disappear like rats from a burning ship. Looking over the equipment and the couch where he remembered lying, he picked up the empty ampoule from the kidney dish next to the syringes. "That's it Mike!" said Mark confidently. "I remember - Jim . . . Hey! Where *is* Jim?"

Michael hesitated before answering, which indicated something bad had happened.

"Where *is* Jim damn you!" Mark demanded.

"Craig blew his head off!" he said in his croaky whispered voice.

"Why? Why? for God's sake?" Mark sat down stunned at the news.

"He was stupid enough to make Grant look a fool. Jim went for him. Had him on the floor Craig told me. Craig heard Grant screaming, went in and shot Jim. That's all I know. I was out digging a quarter of a mile or so away. The first I knew about it was when Craig rushed up to me and said that Grant was under Jim's body." Michael filled in all the gruesome details.

"I'm bloody glad I was unconscious I can tell you!"

"I had to clear the hellish mess away!" Michael reminded him.

126

"Yes, I'm sorry, that must have been terrible; I shouldn't have joked," apologised Mark.

"Craig refused to help, and Grant was too busy throwing-up to care. Craig had the gun and I did the dirty-work." Michael looked ill at the thought of it all.

"You said you were digging?"

"That was for your graves!" remarked Michael grimly.

Mark turned back to study the ampoule. He remembered Jim flashing a light at him, but nothing after that. Mark was stricken with horror when he realised what had happened.

"What the hell am I going to do now?" said Michael, looking worried to death. "I was blackmailed into this; not like Jim and the others doing it for the money!"

"Being blackmailed into it should put you in the clear. I'll certainly put in a good word, assuming we make it back to civilization!"

"They'd got on to Grant to arrange for someone else to be here who had medical training, and I was already known to Grant from years back, and Bruensen; we were together at that time in MI5. Grant was usually called in if there was any dirty-work like this to be done; he wasn't afraid to kill if the price was right. Him and Craig - I don't know where *he* came from. Grant had a lot of contacts, as you can imagine in a job like that! Bruensen, and then later myself, left for civi-street, we'd done our share in that line of work. It was about three months later that Grant puts in an appearance at my home in Bromley. He'd got it into his head that I knew something about one or two of his shady deals outside of MI5. In fact I didn't know about anything - it pays to keep your nose well out of others' business. To make sure I did keep my mouth shut in any event, he stuck a hat-pin into my throat. I survived except for the voice, and I swear he still keeps that hat-pin in his bloody bowler!"

"He wore a bowler even then, all those years ago?"

"Yup! It's his trademark if you like; that and the pin-stripe suit. That bloody stick of his though - that's something recent. You haven't asked about his voice."

"I guess he was born that way!" Mark surmised.

"His genitals were removed when he crossed a bloke over a deal - he thought he could handle him! That's what made him such a sadistic bastard, he plays on it; the suit and bowler were added for effect," Michael explained. "Anyway, when he wanted someone for this job, I was easy pickings . . . he said he'd take out my little girl. I couldn't risk that for anything. It didn't matter about me so much, but not my Sally." He wiped a tear from the corner of his eye.

"Thank you for telling me all that," said Mark. "I hope everything goes well for you now. I'm sure you've nothing to worry about from the law. Grant and his gun-toting side-kick will soon be behind bars for a long time, long enough for your peace of mind.

*   *   *

Outside the building Mark looked around.

"Now where does this track lead us out to?"

"It joins up with a concrete roadway that's part of the army training ground. The labs are theirs too," replied Michael, looking up and down the roadway.

"How the dickens did Grant swing that one?"

"He knows a lot of people and money talks, it's as simple as that!"

"My God! He's a character I don't want to mess with again. How far are we from the public highway?" Mark asked agitatedly.

"Not far," Michael reassured him. "Not if we cut across through those trees and follow the barbed-wire fence." He pointed to an opening in a line of Scots Pine on the other side of the road. Michael led the way with Mark close behind, scanning every tree.

"Are the army on exercise manoeuvres at the moment Mike?" Sweat forming on his brow, convinced he was in some crack-shot's sights.

"I haven't heard anything; but that doesn't mean a thing. They creep about all over this area."

"Oh! Thanks Mike, I feel a whole lot better now!"

They emerged on a small access road leading to the main public road. After trudging for what seemed like miles, they came to a small cottage which had a telephone wire running to it. The old lady who gradually opened the door on its chain accepted the fiver Mark was offering to her through the crack. They could use the phone on condition she put it out onto the window sill - she wasn't going to let them inside at any price - they hadn't seen how they looked!

CHAPTER THIRTEEN

DILEMMA

The police eventually arrived and Mark tried to explain about his kidnapping, Michael's blackmailing, the two bodies they'd find and the two villains on the run. This was all too much for the two officers concerned who promptly radioed for assistance! By the end of that day both men had poured out most of the unlikely story to the officers interviewing them at Parkside police station. He gave the telephone numbers they should ring in order to sort things out enough for him to leave. They wanted Michael to remain longer to explain all the details he knew about the gang, since in their eyes, he was one of them. Absolutely no mention about a possible A-bomb in the bowels of the Kremlin nor secret service involvement left their lips; they'd come to that agreement during their long trek to find a phone. Anyway, they wouldn't have believed a word! That part of the affair would have to be sorted out a bit later on.

That night, Mark eventually arrived back at Bateman street. He looked up at the flat windows - no lights. Where was Jane? His neighbours were pleased to see him and managed to get him into his flat. To his utter relief he was told of Jane's decision to travel to London in case she was in danger. The next telephone call was the one he would remember for the rest of his days. It was a call to his mother's house in Hampstead where he was sure Jane was staying.

An ecstatic Rosemary answered and brought Jane to the phone. She broke down in tears of relief to hear his voice - she had been convinced he was dead. She told Mark how she had left the flat soon after the abduction as she dare not stay there or say anything in case it endangered their lives. She had travelled straight to London and then on to his mother's house on the first available train. She explained how she needed to be in a safe position until she could somehow find out more. She had not spoken to anyone about their work. The hospital had no idea what had happened to the three of them, only that a few people near the flat that night had gone to the window because of the commotion in the street after the crash. They thought they must know the people in the other car and left it at that. The police had apparently arrived shortly after Jane had gone, and she only had a short walk to the rail-station from there.

The very next day Mark took the same train journey to be with Jane and his mother, and of course dear Rosemary and David. It was a wonderful weekend for them all. On the Saturday they spent the whole day in the garden with glorious weather. The Sunday was spent on a trip down the Thames. They had all convinced dear Alice that she must come out with them to make it another perfect day; she did, and it was!

They had arrived back at the house late in the afternoon. Alice was in desperate need of a nap so Mark and Jane left David and Rosemary chatting in the garden as they went inside and up to Mark's room.

"Mark! What on earth are we going to do about the bomb?" questioned Jane.

"I've tried not to think about it over the last two or three days – it's just so wonderful our nightmare's over."

"But that's just it, Mark. It isn't over. We know damn well there's an atom bomb under the Kremlin, especially from the evidence you've told me about this Grant fellow. It was admitted to be a fact . . . wasn't it Mark? Look at me!"

Mark had lowered his head in despair. "I don't want anything else to do with it; I think we've both had enough, don't you?"

"Certainly! But we can't leave it like this . . . hanging in mid-air . . . in limbo! People's lives may depend on what we know; it could even start bloody World War Three. Mark! It could . . . couldn't it? For Christ's sake look at me!"

Mark looked up and into Jane's worried eyes. He didn't want it to be like this, still marring their relationship. All he wanted was to forget the whole thing, if ever he could, even his marvellous invention, and return to a normal life.

"Jane!" he said suddenly. "The machine . . . the bloody dream machine! It's still there in that lab I told you about. I should have destroyed it before I left!"

"It won't matter if they do think it's a special set-up - only you know how to work the thing!"

"Don't you believe it! There's some pretty smart people about. Besides there are others who know what it does: Grant knows. Mike knows. Jane, that maniac Grant murdered a good doctor, even though he was a mercenary. And Carl . . . poor Carl . . . they kicked him to death Jane. Oh my God! It's just not true. It's just unbelievable!"

"It's for Carl and your doctor friend that we must see this through - yes *we*, Mark, *we*."

"Right. You're right!" agreed Mark. "I was just sticking my head in the sand hoping it would all go away."

Jane could see how shattered he was after all he had gone through. She knew full well that he had survived against tremendous odds at the hands of the evil Grant. She swore there and then to kill Grant one day - one day she might get the chance to do just that! It was owed to her. She cursed his name over and over again.

Jane continued: "Mark! Listen to me! All that has to be done is to tell the authorities to check it out and look for the bomb!"

"But, my dear Jane, it's not as simple as that! Think about it. It was secret services who engineered the whole plot. They mustn't know we know, or we'll end up like poor bloody Frazer and Davenport did - silenced! They'll do anything, and I mean anything, to ensure this secret is kept secret. They've got to; it's a terrible thing they've done." He thought for a moment. "What needs to be done, is to get the bomb out without anyone knowing. It can be done, it must be done, or we can't rest."

"Now, the difficult bit," said Jane grimly. "Who do we tell? Who can we ever know to trust?" She remained deep in thought for a few moments. "There is one, possibility just one, outside chance of pulling this off!"

"What's that?" sighed Mark.

"This. Do you remember the face of a beautiful girl which kept appearing in Frazer's mind? We recorded it on video, right!"

"Right."

"Well I've been applying some womens' intuition to this, and I reckon Frazer was in love with her."

"Go on." Mark propped his head up on his elbows.

"Not only was he in love with her, but she could have been the Russian contact who knew how and where to plant the bomb. How am I doin'? OK?"

"OK," Mark nodded.

"If by any chance she *was* in love with him, then she would be heartbroken to learn of his planned death after the job was done, and of course, that he actually *is* dead."

"Yup. So where does this little love story take us?"

inquired Mark.

"It could take us to the bomb!"

"But don't you think it's all a bit . . . well . . . far-fetched?"

"But it's the only thing I can think of!"

"OK. Let's assume your intuition is wholly correct. Exactly how would we ever find her?"

"That is the problem, and problems are there to be solved. Right?"

"If you say so!"

"Someone in MI5 or the CIA knows the name of this girl, if I'm right and she *is* working for them. All we need to do is find out her name and whereabouts; she may even have defected since, for her own protection!" deduced Jane.

"Hey! That's a good point. If she's in the States or the UK, that makes it a whole lot easier to get in touch with her. But how? Through what channels, without raising the suspicion of the organization? There must be a way! We've just got to think of it."

Jane felt pleased for having brought Mark around to her way of thinking. She smiled to herself. Mark kissed her as she sat on the edge of the bed.

CHAPTER FOURTEEN

BREAKTHROUGH

For many weeks to follow, all suggestions as to a way of solving this problem were discussed. Mark had decided that it might be a wise move to confide in his uncle David, and Jane agreed. She knew how close they had been when Mark was growing up and that certainly if *he* couldn't be trusted no-one could! Mark and Jane's positions at the hospital were kept open. Dr. Bruensen was very highly thought of, and as they had important information which could lead the police to the killers, it was decided upon by the Board of Governors to be of prime importance to allow time for leads to be followed up. It was also regarded as a period of sick leave for both of them to recover from the psychological and physical traumas they had been through, especially Mark. As far as the hospital and the police were concerned, this whole business was a nasty kidnapping and murder which had somehow revolved around the hit-and-run of the mysterious patient. They were not told about the link to the secret services.

David proved to be extraordinarily helpful and understanding, although it took him some while to comprehend the amazing turn of events explained in great detail to him. The very idea of an atom bomb concealed somewhere beneath the Kremlin was so amazing that he would not have believed it had it not been for Mark's incredible feat at building his dream recorder and the details of the abduction and the secret laboratory. David knew of no reason at all for him to have made up this incredible story, fully backed up by Jane's contribution to the facts. Then came a stroke of luck which was to provide them with enough evidence to allow them to continue their quest. A news item carried by one of the daily papers from a political reporter in New York proved most interesting to David. It read:

Young woman, late twenties, gunned down in Manhattan street early today. N.Y. police department following a tip-off that she may have been targeted as a Russian agent. Her attackers were driving a red Mercedes saloon later found abandoned. Woman seriously injured under police protection at unnamed hospital.

Could this possibly be the agent Frazer had met; another assassination attempt to prevent a key agent from speaking? It was a long-shot, especially as Mark couldn't remember the face on the tape clearly. Jane came up with the solution.

"We don't have to remember what she looked like!" she confidently stated.

"How else could we know she was the agent?" asked Mark.

"Easy! I kept the video tape with her face, and it had those murky images of that tunnel place on it as well."

"You mean you deliberately kept a piece of evidence which could have got us both killed!" Mark shouted. "Brilliant!" he beamed. "Where is it?"

Jane disappeared to the room set aside for her stay at the house and came back clutching a book, except it wasn't a book. To Mark and David's surprise, concealed within the dust-cover was a video cassette. She explained that she felt so guilty for keeping it that she had hidden this very special 'book' in amongst scores of others in the library room Mark's father had used when he was alive.

Excitedly, Mark pulled out the recorder from under the TV table and blew away the accumulated dust, placing the cassette in the machine and set it to 'play'. The recorded sequences had been suitably slowed down at source to produce images on the screen remaining long enough to study. He hoped this was the tape with the very clear image of the girl. It was. Jane had particularly selected this recording due to the clarity of the images, especially because of the girl's face sequence.

"Did you keep just the one tape out of the dozens we'd collected?" asked Mark curiously.

"Yes, of course, because the girl's face must have been important to Frazer, otherwise he wouldn't have been thinking of it so often," explained an enthusiastic Jane. "*This* tape had really clear pictures of her, so I kept it!" she exclaimed proudly. After a while that clear-faced image appeared on the screen.

"If that *is* the same girl who was shot in New York, then we're on to something," added David.

David's latest toy, as Rosemary would put it, was a rather sophisticated looking Polaroid camera. After a few adjustments on the camera and to the still-frame facility on the video machine to get a good image, David took a series of exposures to record the face at its best.

"There we are," he said, offering the pictures for Mark to see. "They're not too bad are they. The detail has come out well enough to recognise her."

Uncle David carefully packed away the camera and put it back into the cupboard.

"Right! The big question now, is are we taking these pictures over to New York to somehow find the girl; I suppose with the help of the police as they are guarding her." Mark looked doubtful.

"It's a chance too good to throw away, as it *might* be her. If we don't check it out now, while we roughly know where she is, it would be too much to live with the not knowing," pointed out Jane.

"But Jane! How the hell are we going to afford to go over to New York on this long-shot?" said Mark still looking doubtful.

Alice was sitting over in the corner of the room looking out of the window towards the summerhouse.

"I've got a few thousand stashed away," she said, "use that!"

All heads turned to where Alice was sitting. They didn't realise that she understood what they were talking about; she usually let conversation drift over her head.

"Alice," said Jane comfortingly, "we couldn't use that; it's put by for your old age - for a rainy day as they say."

"Don't be ridiculous girl," she snapped. "I *am* old. This *is* my old age!" She looked up out of the window and laughed. "And it *is* a rainy day!"

It was a rare occasion for Alice to laugh, and they all laughed with her. David made a suggestion.

"If we let Alice just pay for half of the costs, I'll pay the rest. Things have been going quite well just lately on the business side of things and I'm certainly not short of a bit of the old cash just now. Shall we do it like that then? What do you think?" He turned to Mark, who was still worried.

"I feel guilty about this money. I'm the one who should be footing the bill for the journey, but the truth is we've hardly a penny at the moment with both of us away from work, and I'm also having to pay the rent on the flat while we're away, otherwise we'd have nowhere to go back to in Cambridge."

"Mark," said David, looking straight into his eyes. "Don't you think you've been through enough? You deserve someone looking after things for you now, at least until this whole thing resolves itself and blows over."

"Well I think it's a great idea," chipped in Rosemary. "This thing's obviously got to be sorted out once and for all or none of us will rest!"

Mark and Jane had certainly not intended for this problem to have overflowed to involve the rest of the family at the house, but conversation became difficult to limit to just David, and some explanation was necessary for Rosemary and Alice to allow them to know some of it, but not the awful central truth of the matter; it would only have caused unnecessary worry, something Mark certainly didn't want for his mother.

CHAPTER FIFTEEN

EDWARD AND HELEN

During the next week Mark and Jane made preparations for the journey. They had booked an hotel in Manhattan and the next day David drove them to Heathrow. The flight went smoothly and uneventfully and a cab took them to their hotel from the John F. Kennedy International Airport. Jane made a quick call back to Hampstead to confirm their safe arrival and then they both set about the business of deciding how best to tackle the problem of locating the girl in David's photographs, if indeed by a stroke of luck she *was* the agent employed to help the luckless Nathan Frazer.

It occurred to them that being in the medical profession as they were, as doctor and nurse from the well known Addenbrooke's teaching hospital in the city of Cambridge, England, it may just work in their favour as a way of finding the particular hospital the woman victim was being treated; the difficulty was knowing where to ask, and for what reason! They had with them all the relevant papers, names and phone numbers they might require, including the name and address of a fellow medical student Mark had befriended at Cambridge. This doctor was now an influential name in the field of bone disease and related blood disorders. He could well be their key into the US hospital system.

*   *   *

The pace of living in New York appalled them. Everyone racing around as if there was no tomorrow. Dominating skyscraper buildings amidst streets of seething thousands and a place where car horns wore out before the clutches. From the down-and-outs to the up-and-offs; every colour, race and creed, milling and swirling about in a human slurry.

They decided it would be best to try to contact Mark's old acquaintance, Dr. Edward Rayner. Years ago, when he was over in England attending a conference in Edinburgh, he had called Mark on the phone when he was working at one of the London hospitals. He had told Mark that he'd do his best to get down there to see him if the conference wasn't too long-winded, but if not, to look him up if Mark was ever over in the States. Unfortunately the conference took up all of Edward's time as one thing led to another, and he had written to him on his return to apologise. A call to his last known address in Ontario revealed that he had started a small specialist hospital unit just south of Lakewood, New

Jersey, about fifty miles south of New York city. Mark eventually contacted him and was invited to visit, so arranged a hire car for the trip down from New York.

Out of the Big Apple it was more of a holiday atmosphere for them, in sharp contrast to a mission to maintain world peace! Their journey took them through a beautiful wooded region and on past Lakewood. Mark stopped the car to consult the directions given to him over the phone and it wasn't long before they turned the corner which brought the hospital area into view. Edward had his house built at the edge of the grounds with a driveway lined with all kinds of trees and shrubs. They pulled up outside the main entrance and few moments later Edward came down the shallow wide steps to greet them.

"Mark, how wonderful to see you again," he enthused, shaking his hand. "And Jane, isn't it?" She nodded. "Do come in." He led the way up the steps and into a spacious hallway, bedecked with exotic trailing plants and colourful creepers.

"You must love plants," Jane commented, rather stating the obvious.

"Oh yes! I do, passionately; it's my hobby, I love to have them surround me."

They continued on into the living area. The ceiling was all glass, pouring sunlight onto yet more luscious verdant foliage.

"I'll fetch my wife. Do sit down, I won't be a moment." Edward disappeared into the tiled passageway towards the kitchen and returned a minute or so later leading his wife by the hand.

"Do meet Helen, my wife. In fact it seems very strange for me to say 'my wife' as we only married five weeks tomorrow."

"Many congratulations to you both," said Mark, unable to take his eyes off an utterly stunning Helen. Her thick black hair cascaded down her cheesecloth shirt and reached down to a delectable bottom poured into faded Levis; she was barefoot and as natural and refreshing as the exotic flora around her.

"Hello," she said, as they both went over to one of many identical blue couches exquisitely placed amongst the greenery, the tallest plants reaching the glass roof twenty feet above their heads and angled towards the afternoon sun.

"Hi!" answered Mark, the tone of the greeting being entirely unfamiliar to Jane; his interest in Helen had not escaped her.

Edward was not at all as Mark had remembered him. He wore an immaculate grey suit with an open-necked beige shirt and pale grey suede shoes. He wore his blonde hair on the long side with curls overlapping his collar and spoke with a kind of Swedish accent. He leant forwards on the couch to speak.

"Mark, where have you both been staying?" His expression changing to concern.

"We flew in to New York and stayed at an hotel overlooking Central Park," explained Mark. "We've come over here to try and see a patient who's in a hospital somewhere. The problem is that we don't know her name or which hospital she's at. This must seem strange!" he added apologetically. "As I explained in my call, all we've got to go on is a newspaper report and some photos!"

"Well, it does a little, but I'm sure there's a very good reason for finding out!" said Edward understandingly.

"There sure is!" Mark confirmed. "I would dearly love to discuss the whole complicated affair with you . . ." Mark hesitated, rather embarrassed. "But at the moment . . . if it were possible for you to pull some strings, as it were, I would be eternally grateful."

"Hah! Eternity is a very long time Mark; don't you worry I'll pull some strings for you as a personal favour. I want you both to thoroughly enjoy yourselves while you're over here. I will find out what you want to know, no questions asked. OK?" He smiled reassuringly at both of them.

"Thank you!" replied Mark. "It is very important."

"I'm sure it is Mark. Now, have you both eaten?"

They had to admit that the journey had whipped up a rather unexpected appetite even though they thought they'd packed enough snacks.

"How about a salad? or perhaps you would prefer something hot?" He exchanged glances with them both in anticipation of a reply. Mark looked to Jane for her to choose.

"A salad would be lovely," said Jane. Mark nodded,

and turned to smile at Helen. She held Mark's attention with her eyes as she returned the smile.

Edward and Helen went along the plant-lined passageway which led to the kitchen. Edward called back.

"Mark! Do have a look at the papers on my desk; it's what I've been up to these last few years!"

"Right! I will," replied Mark, glancing around the spacious 'greenhouse' for a desk. He walked over to the far corner where Edward had his work set out on a huge desk. The massive window facing him commanded a stunning view of a shallow valley, which swept away and down into meadowland flanking a large lake - a dream vista if ever there was one! Mark heard Helen return and start to chat with Jane.

He looked at the papers and various notes strewn across the desk. They were mainly academic papers which had been published over the last few years or so, concerning an area of medicine involving methods of detecting and treating bone and bone marrow disorders and disease with emphasis on types of arthritis and ageing effects on bone, right through to haematological conditions arising from diseased bone marrow causing leukaemia. An absolute mass of work which reflected Edward's dedication to achieve the final eradication of these conditions.

Mark spent quite some time reading this work, while in the background he was aware of the two women chatting. A loud call from the direction of the kitchen tore away his concentration:

"Grub up!" called Edward, something Mark hadn't heard since his college days. He went over to where Helen and Jane were sitting and they all set off along the passageway, the aroma of fresh vegetables assailing their nostrils.

"Smells great!" complemented Mark. "I didn't know you were into things culinary?"

"Come on," came the reply as they entered the dining area adjacent to the kitchen. "It's only a washing and chopping exercise - I'm not cooking!"

Nevertheless, Edward had prepared a wonderful aesthetic selection of vegetables, including radishes impaled on cocktail sticks stuck into half a grapefruit! They all chatted away whilst they ate and later returned to the living room. Mark and Jane were invited to stay the night, indeed for as long as they wished.

During the evening Edward excused himself to make some telephone calls in the quiet of his study at the far end of the house. He'd previously told Mark of his many friends and contacts he had made in a great many hospitals and clinics, especially in New York state and the surrounding area. He frequently travelled to California for conferences and conventions and delivered lectures to medical students. He also provided refresher courses for doctors and general practitioners as well as hospital doctors and surgeons. He'd once given a talk at Addenbrooke's and was promptly asked back to give another if he was ever back in England!

Mark and Jane spent the time speaking with Helen, trying to explain what it was like in England. She hoped to accompany Edward the next time he visited over there. A good hour later Edward joined them.

"I've spoken to some of my colleagues in New York and discovered some of them know the hospital where the young lady is being treated and I was given that information in strictest confidence. What I did was to contact the hospital concerned and explained that two of my associates were making a statistical analysis of the type and location of gunshot wounds affecting victims shot in New York city. As you're probably aware Mark, the frequency of shootings in the city is high, so it is quite plausible for this type of statistical analysis to be undertaken in view of this. I thought it was quite a good idea, don't you?" he said, looking at Mark and then Jane.

"Of course, I must have complete trust in you both to concoct some sort of statistics gathering system, one which would stand up to scrutiny if your work was to be examined. You understand, I hope, that what I have done is to lie, and in my professional context that has breached medical ethics. If this were to be discovered I would probably be in trouble. You both must think it odd that I've done this, but I'm convinced that you have a crucial need to see or speak with this woman, and that's good enough for me. But, for God's sake make a convincing job of those statistics!"

Mark was stunned at the generosity of his friend.

"I don't think we could accept an arrangement which

put your career in jeopardy, it's just too much - we can't let you do that!"

"It's too late! It's done! Consider it a favour," he said almost casually. "I'll hear no more about it! OK Mark?"

Mark looked at Jane and then over to Helen. Neither seemed to object to the plan in the slightest, even though it would be difficult preparing convincing paperwork in a relative short time. Edward stood behind Helen seated on the couch next to Jane. Mark stared at the floor deep in thought, suddenly looking up to speak to Edward.

"When this matter is all cleared up I'll tell you all about it - it's rather complicated."

Edward went over to the wine cabinet and asked who would like to drink a toast to the success of the venture. As the evening progressed, both hosts and guests, in a pleasant frame of mind, exchanged stories and jokes until the early hours. Mark showed a special interest in Helen as did Edward for Jane. The two women went out of the room to prepare coffee before retiring for the night. Helen spoke first, much to Jane's relief.

"It's all right with you, is it Jane?"

"Er! What's that?" Jane replied hesitantly, half guessing what Helen meant.

"Borrowing Mark for the rest of the night. What do you think of Edward?" she asked nonchalantly, setting out the cups.

"Well . . . captivating, I think is the word," answered Jane, amazed at Helen's coolness.

"No. I mean do you find him sexy? I think Mark's

151

wonderful. You don't mind do you?"

Helen had put her own feelings into perspective, hoping Mark thought the same about her! Without answering either of Helen's two quick-fire questions, Jane looked up.

"Hadn't we better discuss this with the men? I mean, I don't know what to say!"

"You needn't worry about them, they've already committed themselves I can assure you! If Mark had been jealous of Edward's attention to you, don't you think he would have said something by now?"

Helen poured out the coffees and looked to Jane for confirmation.

"Yes. Well I suppose you're right; it's just that this situation has never arisen before."

"Well it has now, so enjoy it! That is if it's OK with you and Mark; Edward and I certainly wouldn't want to cause any ill feeling between us all - just the opposite in fact." She smiled sweetly at Jane to reassure her. "Anyway, when the men went out for some fresh air I'm sure they were discussing us - if I know Edward!"

When the two women returned with the coffees they were met with raucous laughter coming from the direction of the open patio windows. The men were swapping bawdy jokes.

"Coffee!" called Helen, as Mark wandered in closely followed by Edward. "There you are," she said to Jane, "there's only one thing on their minds!"

Mark exchanged reassuring smiles with Jane as they

sipped their coffees. Not much more was said or indeed needed to be said. The cups were deposited in the kitchen and Edward flicked out the lights and took hold of Jane's hand as he placed the other on Mark's shoulder and winked.

The Summerhouse Project

CHAPTER SIXTEEN

HOSPITALITY!

They took the main stairway which overlooked the grand floral sitting room next to the magnificent window with the marvellous view of the valley on this spectacular moonlit night. Edward and Jane went in one direction when they reached the landing and Helen gestured for Mark to lead the way into the visitor's bedroom. Mark was in no position to judge events; he was utterly besotted by Helen and went like a lamb to slaughter. She proved to be as incredible out of her Levi's as she was in them. They took a shower together revelling in their lustful nudity, that refreshingly new sensation when a couple are flesh to flesh for the first time.

As they made love, Mark fantasised. It was as though Helen was part of the whole jungle of steaming exotic plants, like a latter-day Eve; a sexual temptress, whose perfume and personal ambience pervaded his body and soul, drawn to her like a fly to the Venus trap. He thought he could happily die like this. If The Bomb was going to drop, then now was the moment, entwined like the creepers. He was drawn inexorably into Helen's body.

It was possibly the greatest experience of his life, and as his lust for Helen slowly subsided, the guilt for Jane insidiously crept into his mind. How was she? Was she feeling and thinking the same? And, if she was, was it right and correct for them both to experience a new, different sensation? The only danger was if either of them were to fall in love! The bond he shared with Jane had been built upon solid foundations over a long period of time. Helen? Why, he'd only met her that day, it wasn't love, but pure, sweet, exotic lust. He hoped in his befuddled mind that it was the same for the others. He wanted Jane to have experienced exactly the same abandonment as he had done - without guilt, without love - just the enjoyment, which should not be denied to anyone.

The very moment dawn broke, Jane looked at the man beside her on the bed. He was still as naked as when they had made love, as was she. It seemed like a dream to her, a part of the strange dreams from Mark's machine, yet, as the moments passed, she relived the hours she had spent with this man - it was certainly no dream! Jane slipped out the bed and to the bathroom along the passageway, stopping for a moment outside the visitor's bedroom. She didn't know why.

The repeated rattle of the internal mailbox made Mark sit bolt upright, with Helen half hanging around his neck.

"What is it? What's the matter?" said a startled Helen, suddenly realising it was Mark beside her. She smiled.

"Some noise woke me, I . . ." He broke off.

"Oh, it must have been the mail; we're used to it and don't seem to notice it," she said, not at all surprised to see him beside her. "What time is it?"

Mark desperately tried to focus on his wristwatch, and finally came to the not entirely confident conclusion that it was just after eight-thirty. Helen stepped from the bed.

"I'll get the coffee on," she said. "Or perhaps you prefer tea in England?"

"Ah! But we're not in England," Mark replied. "Coffee would be perfect," he called after her as she made her way down to the kitchen. Jane appeared in the doorway. Mark was lost for words, as if some external force was preventing him from speaking. After a few seconds, which seemed like minutes to both of them, Jane rushed over to Mark as he sat on the edge of the bed.

"Are you OK Mark?" she said, looking him straight in the eyes.

"Yup! Fine! You? Are you all right my love?" He tenderly placed his palm onto her face and ruffled the hair behind her ear.

"I am . . . if you are. You didn't mind did you?" she said with an edge to her voice, a sort of pleading intensity, desperately hoping that things hadn't changed between them in those few short hours.

"No, of course I didn't mind. If I had, I would have stopped it?"

"Yes. I suppose you would. But Mark, I couldn't help myself! It seemed the natural course of events to swap with them - did you feel it too? Like a . . . I know it sounds crazy . . . like a sort of biological magnet, intensified by the perfume of the house, the plants, it's so difficult to describe."

A tear perched in the corner of her eye as her voice faltered. Mark gently wiped her eye as they heard movement near to the room. To their amazement, Edward and Helen marched into the bedroom arm in arm, with a large rack of buttered toast in his free hand and a tray of coffees in hers. It seemed such a reassuring gesture from their wonderful hosts. It was meant to be!

"Well?" spoke Edward. "We've enjoyed a wonderful evening and night; we now shall enjoy an equally wonderful day, don't you think?"

Edward beamed at the slightly uneasy couple on the bed and then turned to embrace his beautiful Helen. Jane, overcome with embarrassed emotion, fell into Mark's arms, half crying, half laughing.

Edward and Helen were quite obviously happy, and so were their guests. It was one of those odd occasions in life when an unexpected turn of events could turn out good or bad, and also one which no-one could do anything about. No-one wanted to change what was going to happen, or did, and in retrospect they were all glad of it! Both Edward and Helen were a special type of person, extending their hospitality to the full. A hearty breakfast was had by all: toast, crumbs in the bed and laughter in the air!

*   *   *

A great slab of glistening aluminium quietly slid up and over, revealing a very smart beige soft-top Mercedes. Edward had insisted that they were to see his clinic before they left for New York city later in the day. Mark was very keen to see the hospital anyway, and was pleased at the invitation to do so. The car swung out of the driveway and passed the trees and shrubs bordering the road, which gradually ascended a slight rise with sweeping lawns on either side. Mark spotted what he thought was the edge of a golf course just over a rise to the left. His suspicion was confirmed.

"It's only been finished a month," Edward explained. "A spate of bad weather halted work on it last year; we must find time for a game together next time you're over here. That's a date then?"

"That's a date!" confirmed Mark.

They came to a halt at the main entrance to the architecturally superb building. The whole of one side was in fact also the roof, tiled with scores of solar panels and glass. At the top of the gently slanted glass wall, the remaining seven or eight yards were at an acute angle and made a vast window in the same architectural style as the living room ceiling back at the house. Jane whispered to Mark.

"I bet it's full of plants just the same." Mark smiled and nodded.

"Yes, and they're just as beautiful!" commented Edward. Having acute hearing he had just caught the gist of the whisper, much to their embarrassment.

Leaving the car under a magnificent palm, they made their way up the same art déco styled steps as the house - long, shallow and wide - so comfortable to walk upon. Edward seemed to have thought of everything. The other wall of the building was made of gold-tinted hexagonal glass panels. Each panel tessellated with the next, forming a huge mosaic - an art form in itself. Shuttering controlled the light input over the whole of the glass wall; even the moveable clear glass section at the apex was motor-controlled. Under the roof side were situated the eighteen beds, from one end of the building to the other, each within independent alcoves which were each able to be removed for straight-through cleaning, and which were able to be placed in just about any configuration chosen, including a novel hexagonal bee-cell arrangement, complementing the vast golden wall of glass opposite. Mark was utterly bowled over by it all; he'd never seen anything remotely as ambitious as this place proved to be.

"Edward, old fellow . . . this building is a masterpiece, a monument to your dedication."

They quickly made their way back to the house and Mark and Jane went in to collect their things. After hastily bundling a few last items into the hire car they went to the steps to bid their friends farewell. Edward gave Mark the address and location of the hospital in question and wished him well in resolving the problem, as yet undisclosed to him. Mark gave Helen a kiss and Edward survived an enormous hug from Jane. Once in the car, they swung around to face the drive.

"Good luck!" shouted Edward. "See you both soon." They turned, waved, and set off up the drive, Mark still clutching the precious piece of paper with the address which he dearly hoped would soon lead to an end of the nightmare which haunted them both.

On their way to New York they visited the Edison Memorial Tower; Edward had told them it was worth a look since they were passing nearby. They didn't stay long and were soon heading in the direction of Newark, but turned off onto Interstate Highway 278 and across to Long Island. The hospital was at Garden City, but they booked in at a small hotel just south of Lawrence, a considerable distance south, to organise their gunshot statistics. They wanted their base well away from the hospital in case of unforeseen problems.

"What we need," said Mark thoughtfully, "is a sort of clip-board arrangement with a great wad of paper under a few genuine looking lists and charts, that sort of thing. We can easily make it appear to be normal - we've collected enough data in our time after all. If anyone can produce a convincing bit of stats, it's us!"

Jane anxiously pointed out that if they were discovered to be bogus, Edward would be in trouble as well as themselves.

"One thing we *are* OK for, is the mandatory white coat: slightly grubby and complete with ink marks above the top pocket and various wipe marks on the tails," she laughed, remembering these as the hallmarks of doctors and lab technicians.

"Very authentic! We did bring them, didn't we?" Jane nodded.

They had brought with them a great deal of their doctor and nurse associated regalia, and of course the proof that Mark was indeed a doctor, complete with trailing stethoscope from the side pocket! The rest of the afternoon's preparation went as well as could be expected under the makeshift conditions. Jane had completed a dozen A4 sheets neatly ruled in black ink with all the different areas and precincts of the city tabulated against type of firearm used and an outline of a male and female to which she could mark in the positions of ballistic entry and exit and resulting damage. It certainly impressed Mark, but then Jane had always been good at that sort of thing - presentation for examination answers and such like.

"With Edward's recommendation we wouldn't be looked at too closely," muttered Mark into his mug of coffee. "It all seems pretty good to me; besides, with our English accents they love you. I hope!" he quickly added.

"Mark," began Jane. "We must talk to her on her own of course, and that might not be too easy! We'll take the Note-Mate recorder with us, then we won't have to remember what she says - assuming she isn't unconscious. But then the person Edward spoke to would have told him wouldn't they?"

By late evening they had done everything they could think of, including trying to predict any awkward questions they may be asked, even some innocent remark which may catch them off guard. A Plan B situation was decided upon to enable either one of them to slip-out of any questioning. All was ready.

The Summerhouse Project

CHAPTER SEVENTEEN

NATASHA

The next day arrived a lot quicker than anticipated. Had they thought of everything? As Jane prepared their props, Mark was on the phone to the hospital to check they were expected and that they could talk to the gunshot patients. Their visit was confirmed by a senior registrar and was arranged for ten that morning.

"We've been up this street twice already!" commented a nervously irritable Jane.

"I *do* know that!"

"Have another look at the map," she suggested. They had planned on finding the location the day before, but the preparation had taken up all their time.

"Look for a sign-post for Maryvale Infirmary - a sign might not mention the word 'hospital'!"

"OK, OK! I'm looking!"

All the streets looked the same and the time was fast approaching ten. They eventually found the access road with the main hospital in full view ahead. The car park was landscaped with rows of beautiful lush green trees set in strips of garden beds dividing the area into neat lots. After parking and gathering up all the gear they needed to take with them, they both walked across to the grassy slope which appeared to lead to the entrance. On turning the corner the main reception hall for admissions faced them, strangely though, with hardly a soul to be seen. At reception Mark rang the desk bell. A rather austere senior nurse popped her head around the corner of the door to the room behind the desk, quickly throwing down a magazine onto a chair Mark noticed, reflected in the glass-panelled half-open door.

"Good morning," she said, hands palm down on the desk.

"Good morning. We're expected at around ten. I spoke to your senior registrar earlier on the phone, but I don't know the name of the doctor we are to see," apologised Mark.

"That would be Dr. Freeman. He left a memo asking for you to go straight up to his room. You are doctors James and Ryder from England?" She checked, even though their English accents were entirely apparent! "Just wait here a moment, I'd better just check he's in his room."

She moved to the far end of the long reception desk and picked up the phone.

"Ah! Dr. Freeman, the two doctors from England have arrived. Shall I . . . Oh, right! . . . Straight up now. Thank you." She turned to Mark and Jane. "This way if you please."

They followed her up to the next floor where she then directed them to Freeman's room. Mark thanked her, and as she went back down to reception they made their way along a ghastly grey corridor, two lefts and a right and they should be there! A door in front of them was open and Mark put his head around the door whilst knocking.

"Do come in," a voice said, giving them a warm and hearty American style welcome.

As they entered the room they saw the man who would make or break their plan. He was a jolly, burly sort of man, who right from the start showed great interest in their statistical work.

"Eddy Rayner tells me you want to check out our gunshot patients. Our latest victim is a strange young lady, obviously Russian, she spoke nothing else when she finally came out of the anaesthetic. Do you know, I removed four bullets from her neck and chest and none, repeat none, had caused any significant damage - astounding isn't it - how someone can be so lucky! I wasn't so lucky . . . Still got bloody shrapnel moving around in my leg - gives me hell at times!"

All Mark could think of, was not only had this young lady been extremely lucky, but so had they; she was conscious and able to speak, albeit in Russian!

"Can she speak to us about the incident?" asked Jane cautiously.

"Well, yes! If you can understand Russian!" He was

certainly amused at the predicament. Not so, Mark and Jane.

The first thing they must establish is that the girl in the bed is the same as the girl in the photographs which Jane had in her document case. This they would have to decide for themselves so as not to arouse any suspicion of their true reason for being there. How, for instance, could they possibly explain with any credibility, their possession of photographs of her, especially ones obviously taken from a TV screen when the girl had never been shown on it?

Mark was just on the verge of asking to be taken to her bed, when Dr. Freeman spoke.

"I must say, I'm really interested in your project on New York shootings. I spent some time in the city a good many years ago now," he recollected nostalgically as he walked over to the window, hands in his pockets and leaning back slightly as if to ease the imaginary backache those times had given him. "Terrible, some of the patients we were expected to put back together. No-one's safe these days. It's a bustling city where no person 'cept close family can trust each other. I remember one case. It was in . . ."

Mark apologetically butted in.

"I'm sorry to rush you, but we have rather a tight schedule at the moment. If we could see this Russian patient please?"

"Yeah, sorry I do go on a bit. My wife's always on at me about it - gettin' old, that's what it is. Going on about

168

the past all the time."

"We do understand. You must have some great stories to tell," commented Jane tactfully.

"I sure do. Now let me clear it with the security guards upstairs."

He went over to the phone, picked it up and put it down again, looking thoughtful. Mark took a quick glance at Jane. Something wasn't quite right. Why had he not contacted the guards? Dr. Freeman turned and faced them, his forehead furrowed with concern of some kind. They were sure they'd been rumbled. Freeman went to speak.

"It was in nineteen sixty four . . . that's it, that was the memory that'll live with me 'til I die. Machine-gunned he was . . . a young guy about your age."

Mark stopped him there, with a wide smile of relief on his face reflected in Jane's!

"The guards. You were going to clear us with the security guards," Mark reminded him.

"Ah! Yes. There's no point in phoning 'cos they're not allowed to leave their positions you see. It may be a trick to divert attention. Someone sure wants that poor gal dead! I'll take you up personally - they know me," he said with a husky laugh, quickly turning into a full blown coughing session.

On the third floor landing stood a tall, mean-looking armed guard.

"OK to come through?" Freeman checked. The guard turned to look at them one by one, then stepped to one side. Further along the corridor stood two more men, also with guns like the first. They stood either side of the private room door where all the curtains were drawn shut except for the door window. Dr. Freeman himself, had to show an ID card.

"They'll sure want to see yours too," he quipped.

Mark fumbled for his card, and Jane for hers, passing them over to be scrutinised.

The guard returned the cards and took out a key to unlock the door. All three passed through and into the room, the guard locking the door behind them. There, asleep on the bed, could be the very person who could prevent an international incident and a resurgence of the cold war intensity between East and West.

Dr. Freeman went over to her and gently shook her awake. For a moment she was startled to see three people at her bedside, but not half as startled as Mark and Jane were! They had no need to consult uncle David's Polaroid handy-work, for this was the girl in Frazer's dreams, of that there was no doubt.

Frazer's memory image on the photographs was uncannily true to life, proof that the dream machine really did work! She immediately started to speak long phrases in Russian, completely alien to any of them. Mark suggested that if they sat with her for a while, they might glean something of what she was speaking of, especially with the help of a pencil and paper. This came as something of a blow. Weren't all Russian agents fully conversant with the English language? Surely they had to be!

Dr. Freeman left the room to hunt out some paper. Of course they had plenty with them on a statistical exercise such as this, but they wanted desperately to be alone with her for the questions they needed to ask, if only they could! Outside, the moment the guard locked the door after Freeman, Jane turned to try and communicate with her as best she could. She switched on the Note-Mate recorder hoping the room wasn't bugged. It was a risk they had to take.

"Nathan Frazer," she began in earnest. "Do you know of a Nathan Frazer?" Jane added emphasis by gesticulation. To their utter amazement she began speaking in almost perfect English.

"Nathan, where is he? Is he alive and well?" she asked them both, with pleading desperation in her eyes. "Tell me please, where is he?" she repeated. Jane's eyes dropped from hers.

"I'm sorry, but he's dead." She hated saying the words, just as she had done more tactfully on a few occasions before to relatives of a deceased patient. The girl tried to hold back her emotion, her eyes dampening. "Please," asked Jane. "What is your name? If you can tell us we are here to help you. We believe we know the whole story; that is except . . ." She looked to Mark for an agreement to go on. He nodded. ". . . the exact location of the bomb. Too many people know about it."

She looked at them with disbelief and then with resignation. A few moments passed while she collected her wits.

"My name is Natasha. How have you obtained all this information? Can I trust you? I must trust someone, please!" she quietly sobbed into her handkerchief.

"Look Natasha," Mark chipped in with a quiet firmness to his voice, "you can trust us. Whoever has let you down in the past, you can be sure to trust us," he assured her. "We obtained the information about this whole affair by chance. It's a long story which I'll tell you about when we've more time, but for the moment we desperately need your help."

At that point the key turned in the lock. Mark gave a knowing frown to Natasha as Freeman arrived armed with stacks of used computer print-out paper, a pen and a pencil.

"That ought to keep you going, although I don't know if you'll get very far without an interpreter!" he sighed. "It's a funny old language to understand!"

Suddenly Natasha burst out into a trio of long sentences in Russian! Dr. Freeman threw his arms outwards, palms up, raising his eyes to heaven. Mark and Jane smiled with relief at Natasha's quick linguistic turn-around.

"Well, if you don't mind, I'll leave you young people to converse as best you can," he chuckled into a chesty cough. "A guy in my position should know better than to smoke!"

The door was again unlocked to allow Dr. Freeman out of the room and relocked behind him. He waved back at them through the glass door.

"Phew! That's a relief," commented Mark. "If he'd decided to stay we would've had to rethink a way to communicate with you somehow."

Jane leant forwards to speak to Natasha.

"We have no connections whatever with any secret service, British, Russian or American; we're just a doctor and a nurse caught up in this amazing affair. Nathan was double-crossed as you were. You both represented an expendable means by which to carry out an evil plan. It was an inexcusable act of treachery on both your parts and on the part of the secret services, both here and in Britain. Was it the money and the promise of a secret life abroad that tempted you both?" Jane felt anger well up inside of her as she said the last sentence, thinking how anyone could do such a terrible thing for money.

"It was not for money, you must believe that. They threatened to accuse members of my family of crimes they did not commit and to make sure they were sent to labour camps. They said they could arrange this through influential people within the KGB. What else could I do? I made myself vulnerable unwittingly, by becoming an English speaking personnel of an embassy abroad. Nathan and I tragically fell in love, but during the short time we were together he never once spoke of how he became involved. But I did believe him when he told me it wasn't money. I think he was blackmailed also, something in his past maybe, I do not know. We planned to be together when the job was over and done with, we wanted children . . ."

Natasha broke down in tears at this point, attracting the attention of one of the guards outside the room. They all froze as he unlocked the door and came over to them.

"What's the matter with the girl?" he demanded, looking at them from one to another. Mark's quick brain went into action.

"Well, you just imagine how she feels, not being able to speak to us because of the language barrier," he said briskly. "All we want to know is why she thinks she was shot at!" he added, putting his head in his hands in pretence of the frustration.

Natasha composed herself and began firing some sort of questions or accusations in Russian. The guard made for the door, muttering something about everybody ought to speak English. He again locked them in.

"We haven't much time, Natasha! You must tell us how to find the bomb," said Mark, all the time expecting Freeman to come back.

"I know this is the right thing to do, to tell you, but I can only explain the route up to a point." Mark sighed out loud with frustration.

"Why only up to a point?"

"Because I only went part of the way. I took Nathan to meet up with some members of a dissident group formed in Moscow, according to my orders. We had met, as arranged, three days before. I was acting as one of the many tour guides at the Kremlin for foreign visitors. We managed to spend time together without raising suspicion - we also spent a night together."

"I'm sorry," Jane interjected, "I know how you must feel."

"There were two men and an older woman," Natasha continued, wiping away a tear. "They knew of the secret way into the base of the Kremlin itself, through some sort of tunnel system which carried pipes of some sort; I really know little more than that!" she said apologetically.

"I knew it!" Mark quietly exploded. "The machine really, really works!"

"What machine do you speak of?" asked Natasha quizzically.

"Oh! it's just a device I had built to help with our project."

Mark turned to Jane and smiled. He certainly didn't want to put Natasha through all the pain of finding out that Nathan Frazer had been alive in a coma while he had played around with his brain impulses!

"Natasha. How can we contact these three people? If they knew that you and Nathan had been double-crossed and that it was planned to kill you both when you'd done your bit, don't you think they might co-operate with us and remove the bomb - *and* if they knew you were still alive?" reasoned Jane.

"I think they might, as they are friends of some of my relatives who are also in the dissident movement, but it may be difficult to contact them. They wouldn't know who to trust. They would easily think they were being tricked somehow by the KGB."

"Ah! But not if you could speak to one or all of them. If they could somehow be convinced it was you, and if it could be done through a communication system which was entirely separate from the international telephone network," Mark added.

Mark was trying hard to think. The telephone in the room started ringing, pushing Mark's train of thought to one side. Jane answered it. It was Freeman wanting to know if they'd made any progress with the girl; had they been able to use any information they may have got from her in their statistics? Jane told him they hadn't, and that they were going to have one more try. He wished them luck and said that he was glad it wasn't him. He put the phone down. Jane did the same and said it was OK, they still had some time to talk. Everyone breathed again.

Mark continued.

"Is it possible to find out about the existence of any secret communication system? Surely there must be one with all of the sophisticated devices around today!"

"Oh! Of course, I remember now," recalled Natasha in a wave of enthusiasm. "There is a number I was told to use if ever I was in trouble. It is some special relay number, I must try and find it."

She reached over to her bedside cabinet and took out a tatty hold-all. After a good deal of rummaging she fished out a slip of paper which was tucked down inside the split plastic lining of the bag.

"This is it!" she announced. "I am to telephone this number - a Swedish number - and then to give them a coded sequence of letters and numbers to check off with their copy, then they would give me their code to check against the one I have here. If all is well, and they believe it to be me, then they connect me with a Moscow number which will then be able to safely relay my message." She put the piece of paper down. "I was told that if I received no reply then I was to cut the call immediately." She glanced at the paper once again. "I was told to only use this call once, and only in an emergency."

Natasha looked up and smiled for the first time since they had met her.

"Will you do that - for us all?" asked Mark solemnly.

"Yes, of course. But the message! What do I tell them?" She looked at Mark for a reply.

"You must work out a brief, simple, unambiguous wording to ask for the bomb to be completely removed and somehow disposed of, and then to arrange a return call to say it has been done. We *must* know that it has been removed!" Mark added. "Only then can we begin to relax!"

"Has the message to be in Russian or English?" Jane asked Natasha.

"It has to be in Russian. But if the message is intercepted it wouldn't matter which language it was in because it would be recorded and interpreted later."

"OK! We'd better make a move out of here Natasha, before someone gets suspicious. Will you be able to make the call safely from somewhere?" inquired Mark.

"Leave it with me. I will do it as soon as possible. How will I make contact with you again?"

Mark gave her Edward's home number - he dare not risk a call direct to the hotel. He would inform Edward of the arrangement as soon as they returned to the hotel, he thought to himself. On the way out they passed Dr. Freeman's window. Mark shook his head and Freeman threw his arms out again - palms to Heaven! After some quick goodbyes they left right away, risking it being thought suspicious they had not enquired if there were any more gunshot victims to interview. Now all they had to do was wait.

CHAPTER EIGHTEEN

THE WALK

The little hotel was sited next to a stream and the owner proudly informed Mark and Jane that the fountain situated in the middle of the lawn drew all its water from it and back again so as not to waste the mains water supply. She was a small bustling woman with short, curly grey hair and she wore a pair of spectacles which were entirely out of proportion to her face, the blue frames bedecked with ornamental protrusions.

The day before had been a great strain on them both and it was a pleasant relief to stand and chat leisurely on the greener than green lawn in that morning's bright sunshine. The old lady was running the place by herself since her husband passed away a couple of years ago, although her ailing sister helped at weekends. The hotel stood back a considerable distance from the roadway - unusually so.

Mark had arranged for Edward to phone him at the hotel if he received the vital telephone call. Edward amazed Mark by still not wanting to know what on earth was going on. Even so, Mark needed to tell him all about it as soon as the situation was resolved. Several days came and went with no word. They reckoned on it taking a while for Natasha to make the call as she was still officially under guard. Then, if she managed to get the message through all right, there was all the preparation needed for removing the bomb.

"It could take weeks before we hear anything Mark; we'll have to fly back to England if we don't hear within the next week or so. Please read a book or something to take your mind off it!"

Mark was pacing up and down the room like a soul in torment.

"I'm going out for a walk. Coming?" he said. "It won't be dark for at least another hour."

"No, you go. I'll get on with the washing!"

Mark smiled and went out the door, making exaggerated movements looking up and down the corridor to see if the coast was clear!

He left the hotel and trotted to the road. It was a beautiful clear, darkening blue sky. He turned left and made his way down the roadway which was quickly becoming a dirt track, narrowing slightly. The houses which had been uniformly lining the road were now thinning out, distributed in ones and twos. Finally, just the track lay ahead of him, reaching sinuously into the middle distance and into rural woodland.

The Summerhouse Project

It was truly a beautiful evening and he wished Jane had been with him to witness the sunset - all very romantic stuff, but he found it almost impossible to detach his thoughts from the intense anticipation he felt for the outcome of this incredible business. What would happen to Natasha when she was fit to leave the security of the police protected hospital? Dr. Freeman didn't seem at all concerned; in fact he hadn't even mentioned anything about the poor girl's future. It was a difficult situation for her to be in: a Russian girl, blackmailed into collaboration with the KGB and then double-crossed, as was Nathan Frazer.

Mark continued his walk into the woodland. It was so peaceful, but he couldn't help himself agonising over the problems which could have such a profound effect on them all, especially Natasha. What, for instance, if it was discovered that the bomb had been removed? It would completely disrupt the US military strategists, who, using an A-bomb as the ultimate in blackmail, could use it as an almost instant first strike capability at the eleventh hour. Natasha's life would be in even more danger than it was at the moment. She wouldn't be safe anywhere, and presumably must proclaim defection and seek political asylum in the States. She would be in the awful situation of having to look over her shoulder for the rest of her life. Jane, Edward and himself would all be implicated if this plot was blown wide open! My God! he thought to himself, and all because of an invention which would have made him and his hospital famous and another first for Cambridge. Oh how he wished he'd never invented the infernal machine.

As dusk closed into darkness he was suddenly aware that he had been walking and thinking deeply about things, totally unaware of his whereabouts. He had automatically followed the track with his eyes lowered and was now lost. Darkness had fallen much quicker than he'd anticipated; it had passed as if it were an instant while he was deep in thought. Looking around him, he could only see vague glimmerings of light, nothing which told him it was a highway or a house. A mist had risen from the meadowland around him shrouding any evidence of landmarks which may or may not have been any use to him. It was becoming colder as the night set in.

He was aware that he'd been walking easily and downwards, and so deduced that the mist and meadow-like feel beneath his feet was proof enough of a river valley, shallow as it was. The sky had been clear blue when he set out, but the mist hid the stars. The woodland he had passed through was now only evident as clumps and copses, too damp for their growth this far down the valley. Why couldn't he see the moon, he thought? It should be bright enough for him to see by instead of this eerie twilight! He had little light of any sort to guide him and he couldn't make out the time on his watch. In sudden shivers of desperation he had even thought of somehow breaking the watch glass to allow him to feel the delicate hands of the watch, but everywhere around was soft and wet, no stone or rocks to crack the glass. Mark was intensely angry with himself for allowing the predicament to have arisen at all. It was stupid of him not to have turned back as dusk had fallen, but he had simply been unaware of the gradual change of light and the environment.

He now had no idea of the time as he walked into patches of shallow water. He tried to sense which way was up and out of the valley. He wasn't a good swimmer and feared falling into deeper water if he wandered too close to the river - if indeed a river existed. Perhaps it was just a very damp meadow and the river only existed in his imagination. Images of Jane flashed in his mind; then Helen; then Natasha - they were all important to him in their different ways. He shook his head. The images seemed to fuse as one, just as if he was watching a recording of his own dream: the faces blurring into one, just as the images of the rail coach and aircraft windows had fused in Frazer's mind!

At last someone was there. He called out loudly with relief flushing through him. He called again and again. Nothing. He had obviously made a mistake; he hadn't actually seen anyone or anything for that matter. There! He heard the same sound again. He *hadn't* imagined it at all: the quick splashing sound of someone running through the mire towards him - he would soon be safe and warm. Mark strained his eyes in the direction of the approaching sound. Closer. Closer. It was upon him. Nothing. He thought he must be hallucinating. He listened to the sound repeat itself again and again. It now meant nothing to him because he had decided it wasn't real, but still, instinctively, he moved to one side as the sound came upon him - flinching. He had to sit down soon - he was close to exhaustion.

He stopped trying to move on. Standing ankle-deep in water he just listened. The sound of splashing footsteps continued unabated as he stood there in the misty darkness of god-knows-where. Then, as mysteriously as they had begun, the sound of the splashing footsteps stopped. All was quiet, utterly soundless now except for the booming of his heart, pounding his brain as if to be let into it for its own safety within. When he made contact with a tree of some sort, where the water felt to be only an inch or two deep, he embraced it while standing and let his hands slide down to the cold water. He sat at the bole of the tree - at least it was something solid and real, a part of reality which wouldn't move. He propped his back up against the sturdy tree and now, soaking wet, he lapsed into unconsciousness.

Coughing and spluttering rudely made him aware of his senses once more, not that they had told him much over the hours which must have passed. Had he fallen into a river and was drowning? He pulled his head upright, still sitting - he had slipped over to one side, his face entering the water. The tree was still there, he made that much out with his numbed senses. He remained sufficiently upright to grab some kind of sleep through the rest of the demon night, partly reawakening from time to time for a minute or so. At these times he decided he was dead; he felt totally numb and nothing now mattered, allowing him to relax his mind enough to drop back into fitful slumber.

He again partly surfaced from his unconsciousness to make out that something was different - his head was above a sea of mist as the light of dawn allowed him to see. He still didn't know if he was dead or not. No feeling came from his body and the surreal atmosphere of his surroundings unnerved him. He thought he saw people in the mist. Perhaps these were people who had died and had entered this strange dimension as he had done.

There was Jane, he was certain of it!

"Over here! I'm over here!" he yelled. She appeared to move on past him, not seeing him at all. Helen was there, he could just make her out. She was not close to Jane. Perhaps she didn't know she was there! Mark blinked into the early morning hazy sunshine trying to make out further people in the mist. Two men came into view looking down into the mist and moving their heads from side to side as if searching for something on the ground. One had a gun! He cowered down against the safety of the tree below the mist-line, when he recognised the pair as Grant and Craig. How could all these people be here at once when he was lost? They must be looking for him!

He reasoned that he knew too much and had to be eliminated. How could he have kidded himself that he wouldn't have been followed? And now he was trapped! Jane and Helen. They must have told the thugs the direction he had gone - that's why Jane declined the walk with him he reasoned. He held his head in his hands and pulled at his dank hair. He further realised that the whole of the conversation he had with Natasha was on tape. The secret was out and the bomb wouldn't be removed at all. But Jane couldn't have been the informer; if she was, how could he ever trust another human-being again?

How could all these people suddenly be surrounding him, but not seeing him? He plainly could see them! If they had managed to track him down to within a few metres, they *must* see him, surely. Mark's mind was twisting itself inside-out trying to work out the truth of what had actually happened. Since things didn't quite appear to be real and had a sort of ethereal quality about them, it could mean he *was* dead and that there *was* some kind of after-life which allowed him to reason, up to a point!

The morning sun shone more brightly now. Mark rubbed his eyes, wondering where all the people he had seen had disappeared to. He squinted up past the rising sun immediately facing him to try to make out the branches of the tree which had been the one reality he had clung to, which may have saved his life from a watery grave if he was indeed still alive. He blinked, and blinked again. Why was his mind playing tricks with him? Was he truly in a twilight after-life, or alive in some bizarre surreal game? Perhaps he had been drugged by Jane - a 'game' to drive him mad so that whatever he might say will never be believed! As he again looked up at the branches of his tree, he shielded his eyes from a terrific brightness. The branches were in the form of a cover above him, changing into a brilliant cloud, a cloud in the characteristic form of a mushroom.

He screamed. It had happened. He was a part of the demonic image. He was embracing the rising thermionic core as if a parent guiding its offspring. He felt the hot flow between his arms and hands; he must separate himself from this evil flow. Pulling, pulling hard and harder, he could not release his hold. A part of his crazed mind needed to hold on to the security of the tree's trunk as his only perceived link with reality, but which was no more! A part of him desperately needed to release it, to be exonerated from this evil arboreal apparition. A voice penetrated his mind - perhaps another part of himself telling him what to do.

"I can't. I can't let go!" he screamed, clamping his arms tightly around the trunk-like core.

"You can and must release!" came back an order. He felt as two people, one good and the other evil, both hearing voices, imagining hearing voices. What was the truth? He felt himself crying uncontrollably - he wanted to let go, if that was the right thing to do. How could he know? His energy was all but spent and his arms shuddered as he fought to release his hold, his whole body in torment as his hands and arms slid away from . . . from what? Security or guilt? He couldn't tell, he didn't know. It no longer mattered.

CHAPTER NINETEEN

NATASHA'S NEWS

After a few minutes had passed, Mark's mind gradually reunited itself with reality. If he *was* dead he felt aware that it was not unpleasant, not the way it was a short while ago. He became aware of a warmth filling his body, just as if he had been frozen solid and was now experiencing a thawing-out sensation. He couldn't look again at the blinding vision which haunted him, which had relentlessly hunted him down. Dare he look? He was now in a state of quiet terror at what he would see if he dared to open his eyes. Like a child on its birthday, desperately longing not to be disappointed at the present it would see on opening its eyes, yet open they must. The moment was there. His confidence had grown tenfold in all but a few moments. He had to know what lay on the other side of his eyelids which were now blanking out reality.

The light was blinding just as he had feared. He screamed a bitter scream until his voice could no longer make audible the horror he felt. The voice came again.

Where had it gone, to now return to trick him? His face twisted into a grotesque mask of hatred and disbelief, cursing what he thought and heard.

"Where is reality, where are you? Who are you to use me in this vile manner?" He spat out the words as if to exorcise them from his body.

The voice returned.

"Reality is here . . . Here with us . . . Just open your eyes . . . Everything is fine. You will be happy when you look and see for yourself."

Should he do as the voice said? Perhaps it was tricking him again as he had been tricked all along! He was aware of a gentle pressure on his tightly shut eyelids, quivering as the muscles weakened. He again felt a warmth, one which he felt sure this time he should trust. He allowed the warm pressure to gradually open his upper lids. He tried to make sense of what he partly saw. With his lids half raised, partly against his will, Mark suddenly took courage and fully opened both his eyes. He stared at what he first could make out; it was familiar to him: he remembered the walls and a picture hung upon it.

Jane raised his head slightly and placed a pillow behind it. She walked to the front of the bed where he could see her. He looked and stared in utter disbelief, but at the same time began to realise he was back in the hotel room and that he was alive!

Mark cried for a long time, with Jane and the doctor comforting him. He was finally released from a frighteningly abhorrent nightmare - worse than that - much worse. He had returned from a point his mind had reached, which by all accounts should have taken his life. He had perhaps died a little during his terrifying experience.

*   *   *

During Mark's convalescence, he gradually came to terms with the distinction between what he thought had happened and what had actually happened. He was told of being discovered after a very long search, a search which was undertaken by Jane and a few good hotel neighbours for most of that night. It was sheer luck he was found before he died of hypothermia. It appeared he had slipped and hit his head on a root of the tree he was found next to, and this had caused him to fall into a partially water-filled ditch running beside it. When found he was talking gibberish! His coherent words had only existed in his concussed, confused and worried mind. He had lived out his fears and terrors in the most violent of nightmares. The doctor said that in his experience Mark had suffered because of overwork, and most likely the weird dreams and hallucinations he had given such a vivid account of, were his mind's way of trying to unravel a series of events he had lived through in the real world, but translated into an horrific fantasy world which presented no solution to the problem either - a deadlock.

Mark tried as best he could to recall the events he remembered as the doctor continued to explain his personal theory as to what might have caused Mark's condition. He reasoned that since the problem was unresolvable, he had tried to hang on to the last shred of reality represented by the tree, which itself allowed no solution, and so changed gradually into the vision of an atomic bomb, this being the ultimate image of destruction, including his own, hence Mark's embrace of it. According to the doctor, this solved all problems rather like suicide in the awake, unbalanced person.

The doctor was not told anything. He was just left to make up his own mind as what to make of Mark's nightmare. He had no inkling as to how near the truth the images actually represented - it was far too complicated. Before he left, he remarked on how common it was for people to go to pieces dwelling on thoughts of nuclear explosions in the troubled world as it was at the moment.

*   *   *

Nearly a week had passed since Mark's dreadful experience, and both Jane and Mrs. Palmer saw to it that he didn't worry about anything. He couldn't help himself thinking that the bomb was not removed and that in fact it had detonated.

"Don't you think that if it had blown-up, it would have been world news headlines by now? Do try to be sensible Mark, we've all worked hard - don't crack now, please!" implored Jane, pouring him another coffee.

"I can't imagine how it happened. Not the fall, I mean all the weird surreal images of the people I love and those I hate! It was as if it were all really happening to me. There's no memory of tripping and falling - just an evening walk - right from leaving the house to the misty darkness. Then there were people – they were everywhere, truly - surely I can't have just dreamt it all!" he said with despair.

"Try to stop thinking about it Mark, it's the only way to stay sane. We should hear from Edward soon, *then* will you believe *that*?"

Jane tried to reassure him that what he dreamt wasn't reality, although at the time it had seemed that way. Mark smiled in resignation - Jane just had to be right!

Sure enough, the next day felt wonderful. Mrs. Palmer popped up to their room to say a Dr. Edward Rayner was on the phone wanting to speak to Mark. It was just passed nine in the morning and he was half-asleep. Nevertheless, Mark leapt uneasily out of the bed and staggered across the room and down the stairs. The phone was left for him hanging down, bobbing up and down from the dial-box by its coiled wire. Mark grabbed it.

"Yes. Hello! Edward?" he said excitedly.

"OK! This is the message I received a few minutes ago Mark; shall I go ahead and read it over the phone or do you want us to meet?"

"I'm sure it's all right to speak here; there's no switchboard, just the one phone here in the hallway. Fire away!" said Mark, hardly able to contain himself.

"Natasha said the following: 'All is done abroad we spoke of, no problems or casualties. Contact me soon.' Did you get that? You know what it means I hope?" added Edward.

"I sure do. It's terrific news!" enthused Mark.

"Well, thank goodness for that! I'm sure you'll tell me what it's all about in your own good time."

"Of course I will Edward. It was just better not to tell anyone for the time being. You'll understand when I tell you - you won't believe it! Many thanks to you Edward - a true friend. Take care of yourself and that lovely wife of yours."

"Ah! Ha! The same goes for you and the lovely Jane. I'll be seeing you," said Edward and then hung-up.

Mark made it up the stairs in three.

"Jane! It's done, it is really done! The bomb's gone . . . right from under their noses at the Krem. Isn't that fantastic news?"

Jane flung her arms around him. They could now start their lives afresh.

"One thing!" remarked Jane cryptically.

"What's that? Now no tricks or surprises. Promise?"

"It's just that I don't know what will become of Natasha. We must go and see her as soon as we can. Right?"

"Right!" agreed Mark. "I think she's still in danger. For

what she and her colleagues have done she ought to get a bloody medal, don't you think?"

Jane remained thoughtful for a few moments.

"Look, if she is able to successfully defect and is allowed to remain here in the States, would there be any reason why she couldn't come over to England - back with us I mean!" Jane looked serious.

"I don't really know," admitted Mark, rather taken aback at the suggestion. "I don't see why not. If she is accepted as an American citizen then presumably all she has to do is to obtain a British passport. I think she would have to have a work permit; I'll have to find out. You're serious about her aren't you? I agree with you, it's the least we could do to ask her anyway."

"She did mention that she had friends or relatives in Washington D.C.. She might want to go there!" Jane suggested.

"We'll have to see." Mark gave her an enormous hug and lifted her off the floor.

Later that day they paid Natasha a visit at the hospital with the excuse to Dr. Freeman that they had written out some questions in Russian to see if that would help with obtaining at least a few bits of information for their written report; Jane already had the bullet entry diagrams filled in. It was wonderful, with everyone in high spirits. Both of them congratulated her for the important telephone call she made and later received. She told them she would soon be well enough to leave the hospital and it was then that Mark told her of their offer.

"I am overwhelmed by your kind generosity - I don't know what to say," she replied.

"Simple," said a beaming Mark, "Say yes!"

"I would love to come to England, but I have a great problem ahead of me now. If I declare defection and was able to stay in this country I would feel duty bound to live with cousins in D.C.," she said, turning to look at Jane. She looked saddened as she said it, which prompted Jane to ask if she would be happy to stay with them instead. Natasha thought for a minute before she spoke.

"The family is not of the type I would be happy to live with as there are problems, but I might be able to improve things - I could find a job. I am well trained in office procedure and I could then help financially and help teach the children. I must help them now I am in a position to."

Jane caught her attention and gently held up her chin.

"Natasha, you are a young and beautiful woman. If you wanted to, you could find a loving man, settle down and have your *own* family - your *own* life. Why should you feel responsible for an offshoot of your family. It's none of our business, we know that, but please think carefully about our offer. In England, London and in particular Cambridge, which we have come to love, you would always be happy. The job prospects for your experience are just there waiting for you, particularly in the universities, and I have many friends. I reckon that within a month I could help you find a good job! You have become important to us; please think it over carefully. You could always return to D.C. if you felt that you must - for your own peace of mind," added Jane. Mark nodded his agreement.

"We will return to England tomorrow Natasha. I want your promise that you'll keep in regular touch with us and to let us know of your decision - that is assuming all goes well with you obtaining a US citizenship. If you need any sort of references - *anything* - don't hesitate to call us. OK! Promise?" ordered Mark.

"I promise! You both have been so kind."

Mark wrote out the addresses she would need to contact either one of them, at work or at home, together with a great list of telephone numbers which Mark reeled off like he was a teleprinter, much to Natasha's amazement. She smiled to herself and then to Jane. The guards outside the door couldn't make out what all the commotion and excitement was about. Their job was to protect her, that beautiful Russian girl from Nathan Frazer's dreams. They both left after kissing Natasha farewell, she wishing them the safest of journeys back to England.

That same day, arrangements were made for the return flight to England. They left Mrs. Palmer at the gate of her hotel after packing the hire-car. Since they were flying home the following morning, they booked into a pleasant-looking B&B near the airport for the night. Mark and Jane spoke to Edward and Helen on the phone thanking them for all they had done, and invited them to Mark's Hampstead home whenever they could make it. It was then, Mark teased, that he would tell them both the saga of The Summerhouse Project. Mark's last call was to Dr. Freeman at Maryvale Infirmary, thanking him for his help in obtaining some of the statistics they needed from the Russian girl and apologised for being in such a hurry they hadn't seen him before they left. He was very understanding and wished them both well.

When they arrived at JFK airport, Jane headed for the restaurant for some food, while Mark paid off the hire car. Twenty minutes later he joined Jane - absolutely starving. He was in the queue for meals when their flight was called over the PA. All thoughts of food left his mind, or stomach, as he vaulted the guard-rail and made towards Jane. Now it was back to England, to Cambridge and a return to sanity. What he would say to his friends and colleagues back at Addenbrooke's he could not imagine. Hopefully he had a job and a flat to return to, but all that really mattered was that he and Jane could at last enjoy one another in relative peace and quiet and plan their future together.

Many hours later their plane touched down with a squeal of tyres at Heathrow. They had little money left between them by now, but just enough to rent a B&B for the night and to hire a taxi back to the big house later the next day.

CHAPTER TWENTY

ALICE'S DECLINE

It was unbelievable, the wonderful site of his home through the trees as they approached the driveway - a view, which on many occasions, he had thought he would never see again. The cab pulled up outside the front steps. Mark had phoned home to say they would be arriving that evening, but the traffic had been a lot worse than expected. It was a glorious evening with the sun flickering through the tall trees, but there was no response at the front door. Around the back, he unlatched the big iron-hinged garden gate to see his uncle David and Rosemary fast asleep on the garden chairs under the horse chestnut tree. He walked over to them.

"Hello. Guess who?" he said in a disturbingly loud voice. David opened his eyes, blinked and shook Rosemary by the arm as he spoke.

"Bless my soul! Mark! How are you?" he said. "Expected you back hours ago . . . must have dozed off."

Rosemary was on her feet amidst squeals of delight to

see her favourite nephew home again. Jane appeared, framed in the picturesque gateway. David yelled out "Smile!" as he took her picture with his Polaroid. Rosemary rushed up and gave them both an enormous hug and a kiss.

"Thank goodness you've arrived safely at last. We were getting rather worried when the time had got on a bit!" she said, looking them both up and down as if they'd been missing for years.

"You both look well," remarked David. "Especially Jane!" he added.

"Now, now!" Rosemary scolded. They all laughed and sat down on the patio steps. Mark instinctively looked up towards his mother's bedroom window overlooking the garden just as dusk fell.

"How's dear Alice?" he asked, sounding concerned - feeling something, but not knowing what!

"She's having a late afternoon nap," said Rosemary. "She nodded off during the afternoon, so I suggested she ought to have a little rest in bed. She should be woken soon if she's not awake already."

"I'll go up to her room now," said Mark with an urgent tone to his voice.

David exchanged glances with Rosemary as Mark pushed open the French windows and made his way to the stairs via the drawing room. His mother's door was slightly ajar, just as she always preferred it, just in case she needed to call out for something. Nearing the room he couldn't help noticing a rather unpleasant stale smell.

It came from Alice's bed which appeared to be blotchy and stained. At first he thought it must be caused by the patio light through the gap in the half closed curtains falling onto the bed forming a pattern. But it wasn't. Mark was horrified to realise that his mother's bed had not been changed for quite some time.

Mark took hold of her arm to gently shake her awake. She was breathing, but nevertheless didn't respond to his movement. Her face was partly hidden by her filthy pillow. By this time, Mark was seething with anger that his mother had been left in such an unbelievable state. Then, without any warning, Alice flicked her head so that she was face up. What he saw made his blood run cold, it was like some scene from a horror movie. Alice's face had changed beyond all recognition. The skin on her face had sunken to the bones, with her eyes also sunken into their sockets. Her lips were dry and cracked, and one corner of her mouth was bleeding with thick blood congealed on the collar of her nightgown.

He fought back the nausea and realised that she hadn't been up there just for a few hours nap. She had lain on that bed for days, perhaps even a week or more! He stared terrified as she lifted her head and made indescribable animal noises, at first in a high-pitched tone, and then ending with a hideous deep guttural moan. What had happened? How did he feel something was wrong when he was in the garden looking up at her window?

He couldn't stop himself retching and rushed over to the window, thrusting it open for fresh air with Alice repeating her monstrous sounds. He looked down to the patio, but no-one was sitting there. His eyes moved down the garden. No-one. Mark looked further to the summerhouse, appearing ghostly illuminated by the distant patio light. There they were: David, Rosemary and Jane. Jane was holding her head in her hands as she looked up to see Mark at the window.

"What's happened to her!" he shouted. "Come up here at once!" he ordered. "Rosemary! You!"

He moved away from the window and back towards the bed. After a while David, not Rosemary, stood in the doorway. He found it hard to speak, resting his head on the door-frame.

"What is wrong with her David? God in Heaven, answer me man!"

"She is completely insane," David said slowly and clearly, for he didn't wish to repeat it. "She believes she is possessed . . . but not by the devil. For Heaven's sake, does it matter now. She can't last much longer." He choked at the stench.

"What do you mean: much longer? How long has she been up here like this?" Mark demanded.

"Nearly two weeks," David admitted.

"I cannot believe you! Why?"

"We thought she might get better - snap out of it or something. We're as shocked as you are," David tried to explain.

"Oh no you're not! This is terrible. Why didn't you contact me in the States?"

"Because it would have served no purpose. Alice would still be in this condition whether you knew it or not. We discussed what we should do right after we called the doctor, and we decided it would be better for you not to know - not until your important mission was over. It would have severely held you up . . . you wouldn't have been able to carry on. As it is your plans succeeded Jane tells us. We told her all about it while you discovered for yourself. There was nothing you could have done here."

David had dreaded this moment, but Mark was calmer now and standing at the window again. There followed a long silence, as both men tried to come to terms with the reality of the situation. Alice was now lying half out of the bed snivelling and groaning in a deep voice - much deeper than a man's normal voice.

"When did it start, David?"

"Not too long after you left for the States. At first she wouldn't leave her room, and then, later, she wouldn't allow anyone in the room at all. She would spit and claw; both of us have lumps of skin pulled away, they seem to be healing now. She became uncontrollable and her voice changed dramatically," continued David. "The doctor came over on several occasions. There was nothing he could do, only commit her to some asylum. Would you have wanted that Mark?"

"No. No. Of course not! I understand your dilemma

now, but it was a terrible shock. Terrible. I simply don't know what to do!" He looked up at David's face: "I'm sorry."

"I'm glad you see the problem. What can we do?"

"You say she is possessed, but not by the devil . . . then by what?" said Mark, slowly shaking his head in despair.

David continued to say how, one morning, Alice was nowhere to be found in the house. She was eventually discovered in the summerhouse, unconscious. He and Rosemary carried her to her room where she then remained - changed into some creature. She had been completely taken over by something which was slowly killing her.

It wasn't until late at night that Mark and Jane unpacked their cases. Mark just stood around in the bedroom and hallway, he just couldn't come to terms with his mother's awful state. On three other occasions that night, he went to Alice's bedside, hardly able to stop himself gagging at the stench which assailed his nostrils. He tried to get her to talk to him, at least so that he knew she recognised him. All he got on waking her was a stream of spitting abuse. On the last occasion he knew it was a futile exercise - she was too far gone.

The whole homecoming was turned into a nightmare by Alice's condition. All four of them walked the house almost in total silence; there really was nothing to talk about. David stayed the night, as he had done since it became obvious that Rosemary wouldn't be able to cope on her own. Mark spoke to their family GP, a Dr. Jessop, late in the evening, who told him about as much as David had revealed.

His advice was that she should be taken into care immediately as she was in serious danger if she couldn't keep her food or drink down; this he had told David the day before. There was nothing else anyone in the household could do, and so the next day arrangements were made for Alice to be taken to a geriatric ward to the south of the city. No verbal contact was possible as Alice was driven away from her beloved house and garden, never to return. She died three days later.

*　　*　　*

When the shock of it all had subsided, the four of them attended to Alice's bedroom. The cleaning-up procedure was an arduous task, with much of the bedding, carpet and rugs in such a bad state they had to be burnt. A massive writing-desk and bookcase remained as the last task to be undertaken in the bedroom: hours of sorting through old papers, envelopes, letters and all manner of correspondence, with the difficult decisions as to what to keep and what to dispose of. All the photographs were kept, as well as dozens of personal letters to Alice. These letters were to prove the key to her decline into insanity.

These personal letters, as they were in fact labelled, had all been resealed after being opened and presumably read. Great strips of brown gummed paper bordered the edges of the envelopes and then other pieces were gummed over the front and back in a criss-cross pattern. The decision as to whether they were to be kept unopened or simply destroyed or opened and read had to be made; even after her death, they were still her property to be respected. But one very important reason was evidently in favour of them being opened and read by the family. Something had caused Alice's health to decline, and a clue may become evident in the contents of these letters. Some of the letters were replies to those she had written to her many friends and relatives; these were not taped-up. It was the letters secured with tape which held the answer.

It transpired that Alice had been conducting an affair with the husband of one of her best friends, well over thirty years ago. The manner in which the envelopes were resealed, suggested that no-one else should read them, yet she was obviously compelled to keep them rather than destroy them. The letters revealed the sadness of the affair - their secret had to be kept. It couldn't be allowed to become common knowledge, especially in the high society life-style in which they were involved. Alice had known the gentleman before she married, but although she loved her husband dearly she was a terrible flirt, especially at the many functions she either attended or gave at the big Hampstead house. Mark's uncle David knew all about it, but had sworn to Alice never to reveal his sister's affair - he had no intention of doing so anyway. He knew of their secret meetings in the summerhouse - a splendid place. In its wild state today it certainly had its own special charm and magnetism, despite its insidious dereliction. The letters slowly built up into a love story worthy of any classic book or epic film.

They had both suffered the most terrible guilt and mental stress, only living for the next time they could be alone in the relative seclusion of the summerhouse. It was later revealed in a letter hidden at the back of the desk that the now old gentleman had died while Mark was away in the States with Jane. The discovery of his death had an utterly profound effect on Alice, and her already deteriorating health went into a hopeless decline. The final turning point came when she took it upon herself to reach the summerhouse, just as if she needed to recall those magical moments from all those long years ago. If she did recall them or had failed to, either outcome propelled her to insanity and death.

David filled in most of the details the letters failed to divulge as Alice had confided in David with the problems which faced her. She had total trust in him, and it was only now, after her death, that David felt the others should know about the reason for her condition and inevitable death. He had only been shown a few of the love letters by Alice in confidence, and knew nothing of their taping-up until now, but Alice *had* shown him the letter containing the newspaper cutting of her lover's obituary.

The Summerhouse Project

Many, but by no means all, of Alice's friends attended the cremation, along with most of the remaining family. The family solicitor contacted Mark after the cremation and told him that his mother had prepared a will when she was quite sane and had left everything to him. This came as no surprise, because John had not returned for his father's funeral, nor as it turned out, for his mother's cremation; he was wealthy and successful and had obviously cut himself off from the family. Mark was always Alice's favourite even though he loathed her lifestyle, but had never spoken or acted in any obvious way against it. He had only ever confided his thoughts on the matter to his dear uncle David.

*   *   *

When all that could be done at the house was completed, David and Rosemary returned to their home - they had done more than enough. They were told they were always welcome at the house any time as if it was an extension of their own home. There was no way on Earth Mark could ever properly repay them. The house was now his and everything contained within it. It was difficult for him to comprehend all that had taken place during the past few months, not only all that was involved in The Summerhouse Project, but also the sudden changes he and Jane were subjected to. They organised the house as best they could for their immediate needs, and began to think about returning to work in Cambridge.

One Friday evening the telephone rang, as it had done countless times over the last month. Mark picked up the phone.

"Hello!" he greeted the caller with a sort of lively singsong.

"Hello, is this the number of Dr. Mark James?" said a delightfully feminine voice.

"It certainly is! Can I help you?" replied Mark.

"It's Natasha, do you remember, from the hospital?" As if Mark needed reminding!

He yelled down the hallway to Jane.

"It's Natasha, Jane . . . On the phone!" He gathered his wits. "Natasha, it's wonderful to hear from you, wonderful! What's been happening over there? Are you well?" he managed to blurt out in his excitement.

"Yes, I'm fine. Everyone has been so wonderful I can hardly believe it," she continued.

"That's great to hear Natasha. What about the citizenship business - how did you get on?"

"That's mainly why I've phoned, Mark. You offered me accommodation in your home until I can find a place of my own. I don't wish to be a burden, but is the offer still on?"

"You couldn't be a burden if you tried; can you really come over?" By now Jane was sharing the telephone earpiece with Mark! "What about your cousins in D.C.? What happened about them?" questioned Mark.

"I must be brief - I cannot afford to speak for too long.

As you must have gathered, I have been allowed US citizenship and can come over to England if I so wish. Isn't that marvellous Mark?"

"Terrific, that's really great news. Go on," prompted Mark, knowing it would be a very expensive phone call.

"I made contact with my family in D.C. and things have changed for the better there; I will tell you all about it if I can come over. I would dearly love to live in your country, far away from here. What do you and Jane think? Will it really be possible for me to do this?" Her excitement was bordering on a plea for sanctuary!

"Natasha. Don't spend any more of your money on this call. Just let us know if you need a definite job to come to when you arrive and we'll soon fix that up for you - it won't be a problem! Otherwise we'll need to know when you're arriving and we'll pick you up at the airport. OK? Are you sure you're all right for money, if not, let us know. I've just been left an enormous house and garden together with a substantial sum of money, so if you are in financial difficulties I'll be furious if I find out. OK?"

"Thank you Mark. You are such kind people. Goodbye, and love to Jane! I'll speak to you soon."

"Bye! Look forward to seeing you." Mark put the phone back on the rest and looked at Jane. "Isn't that fantastic news? Did you manage to catch any of that?"

"Oh, it's terrific news! It's all worked out perfectly. We're sure to get Natasha a job at the hospital, but that would mean commuting from London every day, and there's the flat we're still paying for - what shall we do about that?"

"We could always buy a place in Cambridge until Natasha finds a place of her own and she could live at the flat for a while if she preferred. I don't mean a large house instead of this one. I could never give this up - it's too special!" Mark glanced into the garden as he said it, his eyes settling on the summerhouse.

The Summerhouse Project

CHAPTER TWENTY ONE

BUILDING WORK
AND A PICNIC

Almost four years previously, Soviet infiltrators successfully planted a thermonuclear device in the Pentagon building, Washington D.C.. The high yield device was set in place during maintenance work carried out at a position between two floors, at a point adjacent to an exterior wall. The work involved pouring concrete into a structural support column shuttering with reinforcing steel rods embedded at its centre. A large area was deliberately made available by a modification of one of the air-conditioning shafts and at this position the device was embedded in concrete. Connections were made to a hidden receiving aerial prior to the embedding and the work was completed in less than two weeks. Certain panels were put into position to give the impression that the area was similar to all other areas in the same position throughout the building, thus completely concealing the bomb's existence. A Soviet satellite in geosynchronous orbit had been previously launched and placed into a high orbit position, whereupon it could relay encrypted data streams to and from ground stations in the Soviet Union directly to the bomb's receiving aerial. For the bomb to be armed and detonated, a series of extremely complicated encoded data bursts had to be accurately received and decoded by the bomb's on-board computer. The battery power source could remain fully charged until the signal was received to connect it with, and switch on the computer's arming program. A full eighteen separate encoded signals from the satellite overhead would need to be received and decoded before detonation - a fail-safe procedure to ensure that accidental arming of the bomb could not happen.

This nuclear bomb was far more powerful than the Anglo-American device at the Kremlin - it was a hydrogen bomb. It wasn't beyond the limits of detection, but incorporated specifically designed shields of hi-tech mu-alloy lead laminates to contain emitted radioactivity. It sat there awaiting the signals to annihilate The District, the Pentagon, the White House and everything else for miles around.

The reason for deploying this bomb was for the same reason the Anglo-American secret services deployed theirs: as a blackmailing first-strike stratagem. The difference, however, was that the Soviets thought of the idea and carried it out well before the now aborted Kremlin device was put in position by Nathan Frazer, together with the essential guidance of Natasha and her band of western sympathisers. The Pentagon bomb was checked daily by the satellite for any possible malfunction or discovery. The bomb's concrete casing contained dozens of strain-gauges of the type used in engineering and weld testing for brittle fracture. If any part of the concrete was tampered with or suffered damage in any way, such as an earthquake, the Russians would have that information relayed back to them via satellite.

Not far away a US government research department was under way with a communications project closely linked to President Reagan's SDI 'Star Wars' programme. The work presently being undertaken was to find a way of communicating with US satellites, avoiding any detection or interference from enemy transmissions, either ground or satellite transmitted. All manner of transmission devices, wavelengths and frequencies were tried in experimental conditions on the ground and with a test satellite in orbit. It was during these months of testing suitable transmission frequencies that all but one of the bomb's fail-safe activation code frequencies were tripped. The Soviets were unable to halt this situation, being totally swamped by the barrage of signal wavelengths sweeping across the spectrum, *nor could they admit to the bomb's existence.*

Thousands of miles away in their Hampstead home, Jane was preparing a special meal for them both to eat as a picnic in the garden. They both loved picnics, many of them spent at Grantchester meadows by the river Cam with a punt hired from the local boatyard and moored between the hawthorn bushes in a little secluded spot along the meadow bank. For Mark and Jane, picnics and Cambridge went together - the very mention of one, conjured up a vision of the other. Although this one was to be in a London garden, it was the one garden you would choose if you were not by the river in that special Cambridge meadow! Mark was relaxed, lying on an enormous tablecloth, when Jane called from the open kitchen window.

"Come on lazy-bones, show a leg! I've got five large plates to cart out there."

"OK. I'm on my way," he shouted and leapt to his feet.

"You take those three, and I'll manage the others," she said, feeling proud of her culinary achievement.

"Why are they all covered over?" he remarked. "Is it all very secret?" he asked, picking up one corner of a napkin. She slapped his hand away.

It was obvious Mark was in one of his looning-about moods. Jane knew he was happy and that was the main thing. She didn't want any dark moods to spoil this occasion - all on their own in that wonderful garden. It was late summer, about six in the evening, a bit late for tea on the lawn perhaps, but what did it matter, they could just as easily have had one at midnight. In fact they had decided that on an exceptionally warm evening they would do just that!

The Summerhouse Project

After tucking into the delights made by Jane's fair hand, Mark complimented her on the best picnic food he had ever had the pleasure to eat, and in the company of the cook, who, by coincidence, was also the best looking girl in town. As the evening progressed they talked about their adventures in Cambridge at the hospital and at the flat, and their very first meeting, when, as Jane now could tell him, she was hell-bent on getting to know him. They laughed at the funnier times and at the time when Mark could only think of building his machine. He apologised profusely. Later on, Mark and Jane wandered down to the old summerhouse. It held that certain indescribable magic which was all its own, especially as they had recently learned of his mother's illicit lovemaking there all those decades ago. Once inside, under the narrow beams which supported the roof, now peeling its yellowed white paint as if in an attempt to start redecorating itself, Mark became serious and quiet.

"Are you all right love?" she asked, rather concerned. "Is it your mother you're thinking about because of the summerhouse?" She tenderly placed her hand behind Mark's head and ruffled his hair a little.

"I wasn't thinking of Alice in particular - more about us - you and me." He held Jane in his strong arms and passionately kissed her.

"Wow!" she joked, as she regained her breath.

"I want you to marry me and live in this house. What do you say?"

He looked longingly into her eyes as if his life now depended upon her reply. He felt it did. He could not imagine life without her now. He had grown more fond of her as those difficult times had passed than ever he thought possible. It was painful for him not to be close to her - he had experienced true love, that was for sure!

"Well?"

"Well . . . What?" she asked.

"Marry me! If that's what you want." By now he could feel beads of nervous perspiration forming on his forehead. He still didn't know what her reply might be!

"Well of course I will. You don't think I would have stuck with a maniac like you if I didn't love you, do you?"

They both cried and laughed in equal measure with happiness. Everything was perfect.

"Natasha could be our housemaid!" Jane suggested as they sat down on the ancient boards.

"Oh yeah! I couldn't trust myself with two good-looking girls!"

They both sprawled on the worn wooden floor with laughter that seemed to be an extension of their tears of ecstasy; their emotions heightened at the thought of their future life together. A real-life doctor and nurse love affair. The evening sky began to redden - a time they both loved to just sit and look quietly together.

EPILOGUE

It was lunchtime in D.C. with glorious sunshine as the satellite research communications program continued to stream out test signals. Mark and Jane had shaken the tablecloth and hauled it into the summerhouse. There, as many times before in the history of the summerhouse, it witnessed the power of ecstatic passionate love.

Fifty minutes earlier a jet airliner had taken to the air from JFK International Airport bound for Heathrow, England.

In a split second Washington D.C. vanished in a blinding white flash.

Over three and a half thousand miles away, Mark and Jane were blissfully unaware that at the moment they reached the climax of their passion in the seclusion of that magical summerhouse, Washington District had burst into the grips of a hellish seething inferno.

THE END

The Summerhouse Project

The Summerhouse Project

The Summerhouse Project